THE MORE THINGS CHANGE

A Novel

Angie D. Lee

ISBN 978-1-7328641-6-0 (paperback)
ISBN 978-1-7328641-7-7 (ebook)

www.angiedlee.com

*To every soul who dares to grow beyond the familiar,
to love without hesitation, and to live unguarded.
You are honored.*

CHAPTER

1

What a wild, disorienting year it's been. I hadn't touched weed in years—swore I was done with it, actually—but when the world started collapsing in on itself, I found my way back to it like it had been waiting for me. Like an old friend I wasn't proud to call, but one who always answered.

I know I'm not the only one. The whole world unraveled. The day I saw people walking around the grocery store in hospital masks, it hit me—this was real. This was happening. Like, seriously? This can't be real life. It felt like something out of a movie, only worse, because there was no script to follow and no director yelling "cut."

And the timing? Of course it would all fall apart just when I was starting to find my way again. After Mama died, I was wrecked. I didn't think I'd ever breathe right again. But I did. I clawed my way out of that grief. I left everything behind, moved to New York, and finally—finally—let go of Imani. That alone took every last ounce of strength I had.

And then the world just… shut down.

I wasn't ready for it. I wasn't ready to feel lost again. So I did what I knew would take the edge off. I curled up on the couch in my stretched-out pajamas, the ones I hadn't taken off in two days, and lit up. The smoke curled around me like a cocoon, warm and familiar. I inhaled deeply, held it, and exhaled slow.

And I thought about the last 365 days. All of it. The losses. The disappointments. The tiny, hard-won moments of peace that had come and gone too fast. It all swirled around me like the haze in the room.

And for a moment, high as the ceiling, I could finally breathe.

I had *just* started to embrace being single again— the freedom of not having to answer to anyone. But being single during a pandemic? That was a whole different kind of torture.

I never even wanted kids. Never saw myself with the whole white-picket-fence, dinner-on-the-table-by-six type of life. But in those early weeks of lockdown, I would've traded anything just to have someone— *anyone*—in the apartment with me. A partner, a roommate, a toddler scribbling on the walls. Just someone to remind me I wasn't completely invisible.

All I craved was presence. A body in the next room. A voice. A laugh. Anything to break up the silence that had somehow gotten louder than the city ever was at its noisiest. Every time the buzzer rang or I heard a knock at the door, my heart jumped. Maybe it was a friend dropping by. Maybe someone couldn't take the solitude either and came to check in.

But nope. It was just another Amazon package. Another box of stuff I didn't need, ordered at 2 a.m. because clicking "Place Your Order" felt like a tiny hit of control in a world that had spiraled far beyond it. That, too, had become a habit.

I had never been so shaken by silence. I used to *love* solitude. I used to *thrive* in it. But this? This wasn't solitude. This was something else entirely. The streets of New York, once pulsing with life, now looked like an abandoned movie set. The "City That Never Sleeps" was in a coma, and all we could do was wait.

Every time the COVID numbers dipped, I let myself hope. Just a little. Just enough to crack the door open to what used to be normal. And then, like clockwork, the numbers would spike, slamming that door shut again. Back into lockdown. Back into the waiting.

It was agonizing. All-consuming. Exhausting.

And eventually... it was just *numb*.

Until that dreaded call came—the one I always knew would come, eventually—I hadn't really let myself feel much of anything. I'd been floating, surviving, numbing out. But when I heard the words—*Dr. Wilson has passed*—something in me cracked wide open.

Dr. Wilson wasn't just a therapist. She was *my* therapist. My lifeline. The calm in the storm when everything else felt impossible. It had been almost two years since our last session—she'd retired after her dementia diagnosis—but the news still hit like it had happened mid-conversation, like she'd just paused to catch her breath and never came back.

She had been doing okay, all things considered. That's what I'd heard, anyway. She forgot dates sometimes, sure, and mixed up a few stories here and there, but her spirit? Her mind? It still had that same clarity, that deep, anchoring presence. So hearing she was gone felt... wrong. Sudden. Too soon. And though no one said it out loud, I couldn't shake the feeling that COVID had something to do with it. It just *felt* like it.

For some reason, I had saved an old voicemail from her. It was just a simple message—she was reminding me about our last couple of sessions before she told me about the diagnosis. At the time, I didn't know why I kept it. But I never deleted it.

In the message, she told me how much she valued me as a client. That I had strength in me I didn't even recognize yet. I remember hearing it back then and thinking, *Well, that's just who she is—always reflective, always deeply in tune.*

But now... now it feels different. Like she knew she was saying goodbye. Like she wanted to leave something behind.

I still can't quite explain it. I just know that when I press play and hear her voice—steady, warm, grounded—I feel something settle in me. Some small piece of peace. And maybe that's why I held onto it.

Maybe some part of me knew I'd need it.

At first, I thought it was just Dr. Wilson being her usual self— thoughtful, grounded, always ready with just the right words to calm the storm. The voicemail felt like one more moment of insight, another gentle nudge of reassurance. But now... now I wonder if it was something more. Maybe she *knew.* Maybe she sensed her time was running short and wanted to leave me with a final offering—a soft landing wrapped in her voice. A reminder that I had the strength I needed, even if she wouldn't be around to say it again.

It wasn't just a message. It was a parting gift. Her way of saying goodbye without ever saying the words. A final affirmation that, no matter what happened, I had the power to carry on.

When Gigi called—Dr. Wilson's daughter—I knew before she even spoke. I froze the second I heard her voice. Something in her tone gave it away. I stood in the middle of my living room, surrounded by silence and soft light from the window, feeling as hollow as the streets outside.

"I'm so sorry, Serenity," she said, voice cracking. "I know how much she helped you after your mom passed. I hate having to share this news, especially with everything going on. I know my mother would've wanted me to make sure you were okay."

Her words—so sincere, so heavy with emotion—shattered me. She *knew.* She had seen it firsthand, how broken I'd been after Mama died. She'd watched Dr. Wilson breathe life back into me with her calm, steady presence. Her gift.

I told her I needed some time, that I'd call her back soon. I don't even remember ending the call—just the silence that followed.

And then it hit me. All of it. I let out a scream so loud, I startled myself. It ripped through my chest, raw and primal, echoing off the walls like grief made sound. My heart splintered open, and just like that, I was mourning Mama all over again—*mourning them both.*

The tears didn't come softly; they surged. The kind of crying that doesn't make space for breathing. My body shook with it. My face burned. My eyes swelled so badly I could barely see, barely breathe, barely think.

Grief doesn't care how many years it's been.

It doesn't ask permission.

It just arrives, uninvited, and takes everything with it.

I remember when Gigi asked me to say a few words at Dr. Wilson's service—on behalf of her clients, no less. I wanted to say yes with grace and clarity, but honestly, I felt completely lost. How could I put words to the impact she'd had on my life? Her death had sent me spiraling, tugging me right back into the darkness I'd clawed out of after Mama died. I didn't feel steady enough to comfort anyone, let alone stand up and speak.

In a haze of anxiety and self-doubt, I downloaded one of those tribute-writing apps. It was probably designed for weddings and baby showers, but that night, it became my lifeline. Somehow, typing helped where talking couldn't. Piece by piece, I put together a few words that felt honest, and maybe even healing.

But when they called my name at the service, my first thought wasn't profound at all. It was: *Why the hell did I wear stiletto heels to a gravesite?* I could practically hear Dr. Wilson's voice laughing in my head as I worried about sinking into the grass and falling on top of the damn casket. Only *I* would be thinking about something like that at a time like this. But oddly, that ridiculous thought made me chuckle inside. Just enough to steady myself.

The memorial was the most scaled-down I'd ever seen—thanks to COVID. Twenty people, spaced apart like chess pieces, all wearing masks. It was heartbreaking. I knew she had touched hundreds of lives, maybe more. And now here we were, reduced to a small gathering and a Zoom link. *She deserved more.* So much more.

As I stood there, sunglasses shielding my eyes, the memories hit me like waves. Her voice. Her wisdom. The way she had this quiet, powerful way of seeing right through me without making me feel exposed. I fought to keep my voice from cracking while I spoke, focusing on the words I'd typed with trembling fingers the night before.

After I finished, Gigi came up and wrapped me in a tight hug. The air was brisk, but her embrace was warm—centering. She didn't say much, just held me there. I could feel her grief in the way her body leaned into mine. And mine met hers in return.

Damn you, COVID. Why did it have to end like this?

The rest of the day slipped away without me realizing it. I had been so lost in my thoughts that by the time I checked the clock, it was almost six. The city was alive again—people walking, laughing, honking, music spilling out of restaurant patios. It was the kind of evening New York does best, like the world hadn't been unraveling for the past year.

But even as life moved on around me, something inside me had shifted. I wasn't sure what normal meant anymore.

All I knew was that I'd made it through another day.

And somehow, that felt like enough.

CHAPTER

2

The yoga studio that brought me back to New York actually thrived during the pandemic—something I never could've predicted. While so many businesses were barely staying afloat, ours somehow found its stride. There were a lot of pivots, sure—class formats, scheduling, even our branding—but all the shifts turned out to be incredibly lucrative. We moved to one hundred percent virtual classes, added live-streamed meditation sessions, and surprisingly, our clientele grew. The more the world shut down, the more people seemed to crave stillness. Or maybe just something that felt like control.

So, no, my job wasn't really affected. And honestly, I wasn't worried about it even if it had been. I'd been my own boss for years as a yoga instructor before this, and I always knew I could go back to that life if I had to. I had a cushion to land on.

More than a cushion, actually.

I had savings. Real savings. I owned a few investment properties in Arizona and a solid retirement fund that most people my age only dreamed about. Financially, I was in a really good place. *Thank God.* That was one less thing to worry about when it felt like the rest of the world was on fire.

Living below my means for years had made a difference too. It was something I never wavered on, even when I was married to Dave. Back then, with his app success, we had a combined net worth of twenty million dollars—but I still drove the same car, clipped coupons, and shopped at thrift stores just for fun. Wealth never impressed me much. Security did. And I had worked hard to build mine.

Funny how stability doesn't always come from the places you expect. While emotionally I was unraveling, financially, I was steady. Balanced.

Like the tree pose I taught so often—wobbly in the beginning, but strong at the core once you find your breath.

I'm really glad I chose this brownstone in Brooklyn. At the time, I was torn—Harlem had been calling me with its culture and history, but something about this space in Brooklyn felt right. And once the pandemic hit, I knew I'd made the right decision. The extra room made it easier to teach yoga classes remotely after the studio shut down. I created a little sanctuary in my living room—plants, incense, the perfect natural lighting. But the moment the classes ended, the silence would creep back in, and the loneliness would wrap around me like a second skin.

Since moving back to New York, I'd met a lot of people—warm smiles, interesting conversations—but no real connections. Not the kind that sticks. I was so happy Cynthia and I lived close again, but of course, once COVID hit, she packed up and went to stay with her mom in Baltimore. Her mom lived alone and Cynthia's job had gone fully remote, so it made sense. It was the right thing to do. Still, her absence stung.

There was Kevin, though. Kevin—the owner of the yoga studio and four others scattered up and down the East Coast. He and I hit it off the moment he hired me. There were a few dates, some long stares across tables, a lot of flirtation, and eventually, some mind-blowing sex. He was ambitious, and I respected that. I knew his time was stretched thin between business calls and expansion meetings, so I never asked for more than what he could give. And what he *could* give… well, it definitely satisfied a certain set of needs.

We fell into this rhythm—part-time lovers, part-time colleagues. It worked. He appreciated that I didn't make things messy, and I appreciated the reliable, no-strings-attached release. Still, I'd be lying if I said I didn't want more. Kevin had all the makings of someone I could love: intelligent, grounded, attractive in that boho-but-polished kind of way, and never judgmental. We had real conversations. I felt seen. But I also felt alone.

It wasn't about his money—he was well off, sure, but that was never the appeal. I think I just craved consistency. A steady presence. Someone who wasn't just available when it was convenient or when I needed a quick fix.

I hadn't always wanted that. I'd been perfectly fine marching to the beat of my own drum for most of my adult life. I met Dave fifteen years ago during one of my free-spirited phases. Marriage and children weren't on my radar, but he offered a kind of calm companionship that surprised me. We never did want kids, even after we married, but I genuinely loved building a life with him. And yeah… I miss that. The stability. The partnership. The shared routines.

I've dated plenty—men, women, beautiful souls across the spectrum—but I've come to realize I *prefer* committed love. Not the suffocating kind. Not the joint-bank-account-live-in-each-other's-pockets type. Just something real. A person to depend on. Someone who depends on me. I still prefer living alone, truth be told. I like my space. But I want someone to share meals with, laugh with, cuddle with, go to events with… and yes, have some delicious, soul-sucking sex with. I mean, really—is that too much to ask?

Before Kevin, there was Alex and Imani.

God, Imani.

The chemistry between the three of us was wild. I've never been able to recreate the energy I felt with them. But the way things ended, especially between Imani and me… it still stings. I loved her. And I don't say that lightly. I've avoided looking at her pictures because they still do something to me—set off a fire in my body that I can't quite extinguish. I hate that.

Sometimes I wonder if she and Alex had another baby. Did she ever find out he was cheating on her with Melissa? I can't believe I've managed to stay silent this whole time. I haven't reached out. I haven't checked in. I changed my number, blocked her on socials, did everything I could not to fall back into that trap. Because she *was* a trap. My beautiful, intoxicating, nurturing trap. I'd never met anyone like her. She made me feel like I was spiraling—in the best and worst ways. It was too much. Too much up and down. Too much of everything.

So I ran. And stayed gone.

This past year has been brutal. Not having Dr. Wilson to talk to when the anxiety crept in, when the loneliness sat too heavy on my chest—that made it harder. And even with Cynthia gone, even with the city in chaos, I didn't break. I made it through. And now? The studio's back open. The world is reawakening. Maybe it's time I start putting myself out there again. Though honestly, I'm not super excited about it. Everyone seems a little… desperate now. Pent-up energy, unresolved trauma, bad dates waiting to happen. I just want something *organic*. Something real.

I finally peeled myself off the couch, still in pajamas from the night before. The sky outside had that golden-hour glow, and the city was buzzing again. I considered texting Kevin. Maybe dinner. Or not. We hadn't seen each other in months, and the thought of catching up felt exhausting. But the thought of sex? That was tempting.

Maybe I'd skip dinner. Just call him for what we both knew he was good for. An early evening *dick appointment*. No strings. No pressure. Just body meeting body, for one last exhale before reentering the chaos of the world.

Yeah… that sounded about right. Sometimes, you just have to call it what it is.

And move on.

*****

It was my first day back at the studio since it had closed during the stay-at-home orders. I threw my hair into a quick bun, tied it up like muscle memory, and stepped onto the familiar hardwood floors of Yoga Theory. The space still smelled of incense and eucalyptus, and something about that comforted me more than I expected. I welcomed returning students with wide arms and warm eyes, and greeted a handful of new ones, sensing their curiosity… and their exhaustion.

"Okay, let's start with a basic full-body stretch and then move into our warrior poses," I said, trying to mask the lump in my throat. Nostalgia crept in—to my very first yoga class years ago. Back then, I was nervous but excited. Today, I felt… reverent. As if this moment required more than instruction. It required presence.

From the moment they walked in, I could sense it—an almost tangible weight hanging in the air. The looks on their faces, the slump of their shoulders, the slight hesitations in their movements. My students didn't just come back for fitness. They came back to breathe again. To exhale a year's worth of grief, uncertainty, isolation.

"As you breathe in and breathe out," I began, my voice soft but intentional, "I want you to honor everything—and everyone—you lost this year. But also reflect on what you gained. Did you receive clarity? Understanding? Peace? Did you form a deeper connection with someone? Did you lose a loved one? Did you survive COVID and heal? Did you lose your job? Did you start something new? Let it all rise to the surface. Feel it. And then release it here on the mat. Just… keep breathing."

I closed my eyes and joined them, letting my own breath deepen. When I opened my eyes to walk through the room, the emotional current hit me hard. I saw a woman silently weeping, tears streaming down her cheeks like she'd been waiting all year to cry in public. Another held herself in a tight bear hug, rocking gently back and forth. Then, from the back of the room, came a wail—deep, guttural, raw. The kind of sound that rips through the soul.

I knew that sound. I'd made that sound. The day Mama died. The day I lost Dr. Wilson.

Grief.

My classes were usually made up of women from all walks of life. Some spiritual, some not. Some still figuring it all out. But today—today felt like a full-blown Baptist church revival, like the ones we used to stumble into as kids at the neighborhood church. The sobs, the moans, the whispered praises—all of it felt holy. Sacred. Honest. I wasn't alone in what I'd felt during the pandemic. Not even close.

Every sound in that room, every tremble and tear, mirrored what I'd carried inside me for months. And in that moment, I remembered exactly why I loved what I do. Why I *needed* to do it. Teaching yoga had always brought me joy, even from the very first class I took. But this—this was something else. This was healing, in its purest form.

No one cared what they looked like. No one was self-conscious about the holes in their leggings or the pandemic pounds that clung to their hips. They were just grateful—to be moving, to be breathing, to be *here*.

And so was I.

I had come such a long way. When Mama died, I couldn't even imagine stepping in front of a class. I could barely breathe, let alone teach. And here

I was, guiding others through their pain in the middle of a global crisis. I hadn't even had a single panic attack since everything shut down. That realization almost made me laugh through my own tears.

I thought of Imani. How she'd gently coached me through that panic attack a few years ago. How her voice alone had helped slow my breathing. She was so tender with me. So patient. Supportive in ways I hadn't even known I needed.

That memory settled into my chest like a warm ache—bittersweet. I missed her. And though I knew I couldn't go back, I allowed myself to hold that moment, just for a little while longer, before exhaling it out onto the mat, along with everything else.

And we kept breathing.

"Continue to release, everyone. It's totally fine," I said gently, pacing the front of the room. "This is our first day back, and it's expected that we need to get reacquainted with yoga again. Some of you kept going with our online classes, but many of you are returning after a long break. And if you're honest with yourself... how many of you have actually dealt with *all* the emotions from this past year?"

I could feel Dr. Wilson with me as I spoke—her warmth, her calm. Her voice felt woven into mine, like she was guiding the words through my lips. God, I miss her. But I knew, in that moment, she was right there with me—anchoring me in this space, helping me hold it for my students. And I welcomed her presence fully.

"Remember," I continued, "yoga isn't just a class. It's a lifestyle. It works best when you let it seep into everything—your relationships, your parenting, your self-care, your beauty, your *attitude*, your daily habits. Let's be intentional. Let's choose to live with purpose. If the pandemic has taught us anything, it's that we need to slow down. We have to *be mindful*. Embrace every millisecond—and just... breathe."

We moved slowly, flowing from one pose to the next. We were a room full of individuals, each baring our own souls. But something about it felt collective. We were unified, even in our silence. We were breathing together. Healing together.

At the end of class, as people rolled up their mats and gathered their things, a familiar face approached me—Trisha. She'd been coming to my Monday evening classes faithfully since I started at Yoga Theory. Late thirties, maybe thirty-eight, with two young kids and a warmth so intense it bordered on smothering—like being pulled into a hug you didn't ask for but couldn't escape.

She looked at me, eyes glossy but smiling. "Serenity... your yoga classes have been the best I've ever taken," she said with a sigh. "I'm so glad the studio offered those online sessions when everything shut down. This past year has been pure hell for me. But the moment I tuned into your class, I knew I was gonna be okay. Actually—more than okay."

I smiled, genuinely moved. "I'm so glad you've been enjoying them. When I moved back to New York from Arizona, I wasn't sure I'd be able to recreate that same vibe I had with my West Coast students. But you all? You've been incredible. And honestly... you helped me get through this year, too."

She reached for her water bottle, pausing before replying. "Aww, thanks for saying that. You always seem so put together, but I know you've had your own struggles. I remember when you talked about your mom to the class. We were all in tears—but also grateful. It's rare to have a teacher be so vulnerable. So *real*. I'd been looking for that for a long time."

Her tone shifted slightly—more grounded. "These yoga classes can be a *trip*, honey," she said, half-laughing, half-serious. "I always felt out of place. And not just because I was usually the only Black woman in the room— but because I wasn't a size two, I didn't always eat clean, and my idea of relaxing ain't meditating on a damn mountain—it's talking trash during a heated game of spades with my girls."

I let out a laugh, nodding in deep understanding.

"But you created a space for people like me," she added, more tenderly now. "A space where I could just *be myself*. And I'll always respect you for that."

That moment settled over me like a balm—affirming and needed. I didn't just come back to teach yoga. I came back to hold space. To help people move through their grief, their joy, their stuck places. I came back to be *me*—all of me. And in doing that, I was helping others show up fully too.

And there's nothing more sacred than that.

"Wow, thank you. That really means a lot," I said, my tone soft with concern. "How've you and your family been holding up?"

Trisha let out a deep sigh, shaking her head. "Girl... it's been *a lot*. Chris fell off the wagon a few times this past year. When everything shut down, he had to connect with his sponsor on Zoom, and he just... wasn't in the mood to put in the work. Then work slowed down, I got furloughed, and with the kids at home—whew. It's been a mess."

She paused, her eyes beginning to well up.

"Thankfully, he hasn't gotten violent or anything. But when he drinks, he gets real angry. Disrespectful, too. And I can't lie—he hurts my feelings. I try to remind myself he's grieving. His brother's death hit him hard. They were so close. And his dad was an alcoholic too, so... it runs deep. Chris never had issues until after his brother passed. He's just in a really dark place right now."

My heart went out to her.

"I understand that kind of grief," I said. "And I wish I had a clear answer for how to help someone through it. It's tough. When my mom died, my ex-husband tried to be supportive... and honestly, he was. But I think I needed more than he was capable of giving. Eventually, he left."

Trisha's eyes widened. "Damn. That's terrible. Men are just... different. If they can't fix it, if they can't *save* us, they check out. Meanwhile, we're out here hanging in through everything."

I nodded. "Exactly. On one hand, I'm not trying to force anyone to stay if they feel like they can't—or don't want to. But on the other hand? You left me during the darkest time of my life. You couldn't hold out a little longer?"

I let out a breath, shrugging.

"But we've both grown since then. And crazy as it sounds... we're actually friends now."

I said it with a touch of pride, as if I'd mastered some advanced level of post-divorce enlightenment.

Trisha gave me a skeptical side-eye, folding her arms. "See, that's why you come across so put together. I don't know if I could've been that mature."

"Everyone's different," I said, my voice even. "I just didn't have the energy to convince someone to stay who wasn't sure they wanted to. My ex is a good man, but our time ran its course. I've never looked back."

"So you're saying you *never* wonder what it'd be like to get back together?" Trisha asked, her tone more nosy than curious.

I paused, suddenly aware that this conversation had shifted. While I appreciated Trisha's openness about her life, I wasn't here to be her distraction from it. I liked her—in the same way I liked most of my students—but I could tell she was trying to keep the spotlight off her own mess by putting it on mine. And honestly? At this point in life, especially after forty, I just don't have it in me to entertain conversations—or people—I don't want to.

"Everything has its time and place," I said coolly. "And that's just not where I'm at."

Her eyebrows lifted slightly—surprised, maybe even a little offended. I don't think she expected the boundary, especially given how warm I usually am in class. But hell, I'd already said more than I needed to. And Trisha? She struck me as someone who might dabble in drama—and that's a world I've officially opted out of.

"My bad," she said, backpedaling. "I didn't mean any disrespect."

"You weren't," I said, softening my tone just a bit. "I just prefer to leave certain things where they are. I can't control other people's choices. Don't even want to."

She exhaled and nodded. "See, that's what I admire about you. I give way too much energy to things I can't control. You seem like you've found that sweet spot—being open but still staying grounded. Damn, you should teach a class on that." She snapped her fingers.

I chuckled. "Ha! I'm flattered. But my gift is yoga, not motivational speaking."

"You'd be surprised! My cousin works in marketing and is killing it with webinars and podcasts. I could totally connect you two if you're interested?" She was already reaching for her phone, ready to take my number.

Nope.

"I appreciate that, really, but I'm going to pass," I said, grabbing my water bottle and beginning to tidy up the studio—my not-so-subtle cue.

"Oh, okay. Well maybe we can hang sometime outside of class. I feel like I could learn a lot from you."

I gave a polite smile, trying to keep it light. "The studio really encourages us to avoid developing friendships or... relationships with students outside of class. Just to keep things professional, you know?"

Total lie. I mean, if we're being honest, I was sleeping with the owner of all five studio locations. But Trisha? She wasn't someone I wanted in my inner circle.

"Got it," she said, finally catching on. "Well, thanks again for an amazing class. See you next week."

She left with a couple of the other students. I could tell she felt a little rejected—and maybe she even picked up on the fact that I wasn't trying to be besties. But I'm too old to pretend to want company when I don't. If I'm not in the mood to be bothered, I'm not about to force it.

Thankfully, my girl Cynthia comes back tomorrow. We'd tried to recreate our fun over Zoom while she was at her mom's, but that got old quick. I need her in person—someone who truly *gets* me. No weird energy. No judgment. Just realness and laughter like always.

I grabbed my gym bag and started heading out, but my phone started vibrating in the bottom of the bag. I dug it out and looked at the screen.

A text from Kevin.

"Hey, I need to see you. Can I come by your house tonight?"

I frowned. I wasn't in the mood for Kevin tonight. The sex was good, sure, but pointless. He wasn't trying to connect on a deeper level, and he avoided talking about anything real. I liked his company, but not enough to entertain him tonight.

"Hey Kev, I just wrapped up my class for the evening and I'm a bit tired. Can I take a raincheck?" I texted back.

He responded almost immediately.

"Serenity, it's kind of urgent. Please, can I stop by?"

My stomach tightened. What could be *urgent?* He better not be about to drop a COVID confession... or worse, some kind of STD scare. I *really* didn't have time for that.

"Umm, okay. Give me about thirty minutes. I'm just wrapping up here and then I'll be heading home."

I hit send, hoping he'd follow up with something casual that would make this feel less... ominous. But deep down, I was already bracing myself.

*****

I had just made it through the door and all I wanted was a hot shower and my bed. I hadn't even set my bag down properly when my phone rang.

"Hello?" I answered, even though Kevin's name was clearly on the screen. I wasn't sure why I pretended like I didn't know it was him—maybe because something about this whole situation had me uneasy.

"Hey babe, I'm outside. Just checking if you made it in."

"Yeah, barely."

I glanced in the mirror. My hair was doing its own thing and I still had that post-yoga glow—that's code for sweat. After teaching three back-to-back classes, I didn't feel exactly… fresh.

I opened the door, and of course, there he was—looking like an ad campaign. It was early spring and still brisk out, but Kevin was styled to perfection. A camel leather jacket over a crisp white shirt, dark jeans, and loafers. Effortlessly clean-cut, like he just strolled out of some upscale Brooklyn café. He was a beautiful man, no doubt. Always had been.

I gave him a halfway hug—mostly out of habit, partly because I wasn't in the mood to fake closeness.

"How are you?" I asked, trying to mask my anxiety with concern.

"I've been better." Kevin dropped onto my couch like he owned the space. To be fair, we *had* christened almost every corner of it.

"Okay, what is this about?" I went straight in. "Do you have an STD or—God forbid—AIDS or something?" The words spilled out before I could soften them. I didn't have the emotional bandwidth for drawn-out suspense.

"Damn, girl. No," Kevin said, chuckling nervously. "Thank God. It's not that. It's just…"

His hesitation made my stomach tighten.

"Kevin," I said, more firmly this time, "normally I'd let you take your time, but this ain't one of those times. I need you to get to the point."

He rubbed his hands over his head like he was trying to press the truth out of his skull.

"Okay. So, remember when I told you I was still cool with my ex? Venise. The one who got married and had a kid?"

I nodded slowly, my arms folded.

"Well… her and her husband had been going through some things. He had this long-standing suspicion that their daughter wasn't his. Venise kept denying it, telling him he was being paranoid. But a few weeks ago, he somehow found this old email she sent me—years ago, like, *years*—and I guess she never deleted it. In it, she thanked me for being there for her and said how much she appreciated the 'gentlemanly way' I treated her. It mentioned us spending time together."

"Time," I echoed, raising an eyebrow.

Kevin nodded, guilt flickering across his face. "Yeah. Her husband pieced together the email's date, did some mental math with the girl's age, and decided I might be the father. He basically forced her into getting a paternity test."

He paused, rubbing his temples now. I could see the rest of the story weighing on him like cinder blocks.

"And?" I asked, crossing the room slowly. "Was he right?"

Kevin's mouth opened, then closed. He looked down at his hands.

"Venise called me crying hysterically, asking if I'd take a paternity test. And of course, I did. When the results came back, there was no doubt—I'm her daughter's father." Kevin exhaled hard. "I mean, yeah, there's always a chance when you hook up with someone, but she was on birth control and the girl looks exactly like her. I never even thought it could be me. Fuck!"

It was written all over him—Kevin was still somewhere between realization and denial.

"I wanted to move forward with you—I really did—but I was caught up in all of this. Her husband wants nothing to do with her now. He said he's willing to still see Kari—well, *my* daughter now—but only because he's the only father she's ever known. Kari's going to be five in August, and Venise has been a stay-at-home mom since she had her. Now she's trying to figure out what to do financially. She was actually pregnant again with her husband when you and I first met... but she miscarried. So yeah," he sighed. "It's been a lot."

Kevin's voice was picking up speed. He was clearly unraveling under the weight of everything.

"Kevin," I said, steady but sincere, "first of all, thank you for telling me and not just ghosting me or making up excuses. You've got a lot going on, and I genuinely understand. But let's be real—I don't exactly fit into your life right now."

"I knew you'd say that, and that's why I wanted to talk to you face-to-face. I *want* to be with you, Serenity. I like you a lot. I've been wanting to explore this thing between us, but I had to handle my life first—figure out what all this meant, how to move forward with Kari and Venise."

"Are you asking me to stick around while you work all that out?" I tilted my head, skeptical. "Because respectfully... those late-night dick appointments barely count as trying to build something real. Let's not rewrite history here. We both know what this has been."

Kevin shook his head. "Why *can't* we try now? I know where things stand. I can provide for Venise and my daughter. I'll set up a schedule to see Kari. But you and me—we had something. That connection, that chemistry... it was real. Don't you remember?"

"Oh, I remember," I said, crossing my arms. "I remember being upfront from the start. I was clear about what I wanted. And you seemed into it. Eventually, though, the dates stopped, the calls slowed down, and we were reduced to 'you up?' texts. Don't get me wrong—I was down for it. The sex? Top tier. No regrets. But let's not pretend it was more than that."

"That's exactly why I like you. You're straight up. And so am I. I haven't hidden anything. As soon as I found out, I came to you. No games. No delays. I really believe we could have something meaningful."

"Okay, but what happens when you start seeing your daughter more and grow closer to her? What if Venise decides she wants to try again—for Kari's sake? What if *you* decide that's where you belong?" My voice cracked just slightly, but I stayed firm. "I'm not doing that again. I've already been with someone who didn't know what they wanted. I kept compromising until there was nothing left for *me*. I'm not going back there, Kevin. I refuse."

He studied me for a second, then smirked slightly. "You're cute when you're stern, you know that? And I get it—you're protecting yourself. I respect that. This isn't what I expected either. But I'm stepping up for my daughter, and yeah, for Venise too, in the ways I should. But that doesn't mean I can't build something with you. I have the means to do both. I've got the heart for it."

He reached for my waist and pulled me in gently.

"Damn, Kevin, you drive a hard bargain," I said, a smile playing at my lips. "You *almost* had me sold."

"I'm serious, babe. You're sexy, self-sufficient, you don't take no shit, you're intuitive, you care deeply, and yeah—the sex is *unreal.* But more than all that, I feel like we *get* each other."

Kevin leaned in and kissed me softly.

"Okay but... not to be rude—I'm not really interested in dating someone with kids."

He raised an eyebrow. "Okay. Tell me why."

"I don't want to take a back seat to someone's child. I'm not interested in playing stepmom. I like freedom—I want to come and go as I please with my partner. I want to be the main character in my own love story."

He chuckled. "Didn't you tell me you used to babysit your ex's kid? You even did family outings with... them?"

I rolled my eyes. "Yeah, and look where *that* got me."

"That kid didn't break y'all up. Y'all's mess did. You told me you liked spending time with that little girl."

"Kevin, stop trying to sell me on this."

"I'm not selling. I'm asking you to *consider* what we could build—intentionally. Let's design what we want our relationship to look like and work towards that. I'm serious, Serenity. I want you in my life."

He looked at me with a softness that made my stomach flip. Then, slowly, I leaned in and kissed him—deeply. He kissed me back with hunger.

"Aight, damn Serenity... you know what you do to me. I *want* to take you upstairs right now, but I really want you to think this through. I don't want you making a decision swayed by what I got growing in my pants." He readjusted himself, and I laughed.

"Oh, so you think I'm easily swayed?" I teased.

"Trust me, Serenity. Just think about it," Kevin said, his voice low but sincere. "I really wanna come correct with you. You *know* I can make you cum a thousand times over—but I want more than that. I know it might sound wild, especially since lately it's felt like all we've been doing is fucking, but I needed to get my shit together before asking you to be my woman. So... I'mma head out. Hope to hear from you soon."

He leaned in, kissed me softly on the forehead, and walked out the door like some romantic antihero.

Well, damn.

That was... actually kind of smooth.

Now I'm intrigued—and *soaked.*

Guess I've got some serious thinking to do.

But first…

Let me find my damn vibrator and take care of this situation *immediately.*

CHAPTER

3

"Holy shit! So all this went down while I was gone, huh?" Cynthia said between gulps of salad like it was a plate of ribs.

She was finally back home, so of course we had to hit up one of our favorite lunch spots. But sis was clearly on a mission—determined to stick to her new strict diet. Apparently, working from home during the pandemic had turned her hips into an entire *zip code.*

"First of all, sweetie, come up for air. It's just salad." I laughed, sipping my Prosecco.

"Don't clown me, Poodah. I've always been a little brick house, okay? But these hips and this booty? They're giving unhinged expansion pack. I gotta get this under control before Dennis ends up needing oxygen every time I climb on top."

We both laughed, but her mentioning Dennis gave me the warm fuzzies. If he was still in the picture, they must be holding it down.

"So, how are you and Dennis doing these days—considering you were gone for *six months?*"

Cynthia wiped her mouth and leaned back, eyes softening. "Honestly? We're good. Surprisingly good. Staying with my mom was the best thing for us. It gave us time to miss each other, reset a little, you know?"

"But six months is a long-ass time," I said, raising an eyebrow.

She nodded, smiling. "Yeah, but sometimes space helps you realize just how much you want someone in your space. Every day."

"Well, it's not like we *never* saw each other. Dennis drove to Baltimore a few times to check on me and my mom. He'd make sure her fridge was fully stocked—even though I could've done it—but it was such a sweet gesture. Then he'd take me back to his hotel, fuck my brains out, and head back home. Honestly, it was a pretty great setup." Cynthia jabbed at her salad like it had personally offended her.

"You've got a point," I laughed. "It's just… nice, you know? When someone really shows up for you *and* understands how you need to be loved."

"I really can't complain, sis. Dennis has been amazing. And his family? Cool as hell! I didn't know what to expect when I met them during Christmas. Him being Irish and all… I wasn't sure how they'd take to me, but they loved me instantly. Then again, what's not to love?" Cynthia batted her lashes with a smug grin.

"I *knew* they would like you. Dennis is the absolute coolest."

"Girl, yes! But now I *totally* see where he gets his thing for Black women—his daddy *almost* grabbed a handful of this ass the first time we met. I swear I felt his little Peter twitch when he hugged me." Cynthia burst out laughing.

"That's wild. But seriously, you deserve all this joy. Dennis is probably my favorite out of all the guys you've dated. And that's saying something."

"Same. I'm really digging him. He gets me—attitude and all. He doesn't run when I get a little spicy. And we're both killing it in our careers. He loves that I'm secure and independent, but he still spoils the hell out of me. *And* the sex?" She raised an eyebrow. "Let's just say your girl's needs are consistently met." We clinked our glasses and high-fived.

"I love that for you." I gave her a soft smile.

"Thanks, Poodah. But let's pivot—because *you* seem a little down. You still stuck on the Kevin situation?"

I sighed. "I'm more disappointed than upset. I guess I hoped that once things calmed down for him work-wise, maybe we'd build something real— not just hook-ups."

I glanced out the window, watching a couple stroll by hand-in-hand like something out of a deleted *Love Jones* scene.

"But Serenity," Cynthia said gently, "he *did* say he wants more than just sex. And it sounded like he was being honest with you. I get that the kid complicates things, but Kevin seems solid. Why not give him a real chance? You've stepped into a parenting role before. You helped out with Yaya when Imani was overwhelmed and Alex was MIA. And you're amazing with your nieces and nephews."

"Yeah, but just because I'm *good* with kids doesn't mean I want them embedded in my life. I embraced Yaya because I was open to trying something new with Alex and Imani. And yeah, it was good—for a while. Until it wasn't. I'm not signing up for that heartbreak again."

Cynthia tilted her head. "Since when did you get so rigid? Kevin's not asking you to play stepmom or start a family overnight. He's just saying, 'Here's my reality. But I still want *you* in it.' Girl, you trippin'."

"How am I trippin'? Would *you* date Dennis if this was his situation?"

"Girl, hell *naw*! I *hate* kids." We both cracked up.

"You do *not* hate kids."

"Yes, the hell I do," she said proudly. "What I look like chasing toddlers around my all-white house? I'm bougie as hell. Ain't got time for sticky fingers and juice spills. Now *you*, on the other hand—you're the flowy, plant-loving, deep-talking type. Kids would look good on you."

"Shut up." I laughed, shaking my head.

"But seriously, I really like Kevin for you. And after that Imani mess? Girl, *you* deserve a win. Kevin's fine, successful, emotionally available— what else do you need? Imani didn't know what the hell she wanted. And Alex? Please. He was just vibing off the benefits—getting threesomes with no emotional investment. He couldn't even see that Imani was way more into you than him."

I nodded slowly, the past bubbling up.

"Exactly. His ego couldn't handle the truth. And that shit wasn't sustainable."

"Damn, Cynthia, that's a bit harsh, don't you think?"

"Umm, no. It's the truth and *you* know it. You're just in your feelings right now. And you better not be kicking my man Kevin to the curb because you're holding out for Imani."

I avoided looking at her. Mostly because… well, part of me *had* been wondering what Imani was up to. Every now and then she drifted into my thoughts, uninvited. I couldn't help but wonder if I ever crossed her mind too.

"Let's be real," I sighed. "*I'm* the one who chose to move on. I changed my number. I blocked her on every platform. I'm good. I'm not trying to rekindle anything with Imani." The conviction in my voice was meant more for *me* than for Cynthia.

"Aiight, good," she said, picking up her water like she was sealing a deal. "Because I was about to say—*no boo*. Keep it moving and get yours with Kevin."

Our very fine, and notably *young*, waiter returned just in time.

"Ladies, can I get you anything else?" he asked, flashing a smile that could melt steel.

"Not right now, sweetie. But I *must* say—you're a very handsome man," Cynthia purred, practically undressing him with her eyes.

"I appreciate that," he grinned. "And *you're* extremely gorgeous yourself."

"You're quite chivalrous," she said, leaning in just enough to let her cleavage take the lead. "Confident too."

"Well, I'm glad that's coming through," he replied, steady and cool. "This might be forward, but my shift ends in a couple of hours… if your schedule allows, maybe I could give you a call?"

I had to admit, the boy had poise. Not a drop of hesitation in his game.

"Look at you!" Cynthia teased. "I'm impressed. But I'm a bit too seasoned for you, sweetie."

"You can't be more than thirty-two, right?" he asked, eyes wide with admiration.

Cynthia chuckled. "That was cute. But no—forty-four. Thanks for the flattery though."

"Damn. I'd have never guessed. You look amazing. Either way, I appreciate the moment." He scribbled his number on a napkin and slid it under her glass. "If you change your mind, give me a call. It was a pleasure meeting you both."

He walked away with the smoothness of a man twice his age.

"Daaaamn," we both said in unison.

"Since when do twenty-somethings have that kind of swagger?" I asked.

"I know, right?" Cynthia giggled. "But girl, I'm old enough to be that boy's mama. A little flirting never hurt nobody—but that's all that was. Now he *might* be able to toss me around a little, but please—Dennis got that department on lock." She picked up the napkin and laughed.

"Well maybe *I* should holla at him," I teased.

"Girl, bye. He can't do nothing for you either. You've had your share of wild, spontaneous sex. You need someone who actually *wants* something real. Kevin's that guy. You just need to stop being scared."

"I'll think about it, okay?" I said, with a slight edge in my tone.

"Don't come at me with that attitude," she snapped back. "You *know* I'm right."

She might only be a few months older, but Cynthia always acted like my big sister—and I secretly loved that. I grew up with brothers, so her brand of tough love was something I welcomed.

"I hear you," I said with a soft exhale. "Actually, I wanted to ask your opinion about something else. I've been thinking about reaching out to my mom's old friend Amanda."

Cynthia blinked. "Amanda? Wow. That's random."

"Yeah… I know I was really young when she used to come around. But she's crossed my mind a lot lately. The last time I saw her was at Mama's funeral. I feel like… I don't know… like she holds some pieces of the puzzle when it comes to my life story."

"Why now though?"

"I don't really know. Being locked up in the house during the pandemic had me spiraling. I thought about Mama *a lot*. I was shocked I didn't have a full-blown panic attack. Not having Dr. Wilson to talk to messed me up too. It's like all these memories I'd pushed away started resurfacing."

Cynthia sat back, quietly listening.

"I started thinking about Daddy. About how he used to hurt Mama. I was so young—I don't remember every detail—but I remember enough. And during one of my therapy sessions,

I told Dr. Wilson that I blamed Daddy for Mama's death. Which is crazy, because she died *years* after she left him. Why would I say that?"

"Maybe because part of you believes it," Cynthia offered gently.

"Maybe. I've even thought about seeing a hypnotist or something. Just to unlock whatever I'm suppressing. But... Amanda might know something too."

"Wow," Cynthia said, her voice low. "That's deep. I hope you get the answers you're looking for. Do you still have her number?"

"I do. At least I *think* it still works. Here's the wild part—when I was a teenager and asked Mama about Amanda, she told me they lost contact. But when I was going through Mama's phone after she passed... Amanda's contact was *right there*. I called on a whim, and it *was* her. So clearly, they reconnected at some point. But why keep that from me?"

The silence that followed hung heavy between us.

I stared into the distance, caught between the past and the truth I wasn't sure I was ready to uncover.

"Girl, you're really digging into all this. Are you sure you're ready for whatever truth might come out?" Cynthia asked, side-eyeing me over her glass.

"I don't know," I admitted. "But something keeps pushing me to reach out to Amanda—like, soon. I can't shake the feeling."

"Well, you've always been intuitive," she said, her tone softening. "You probably *are* picking up on something. I just don't want this to spiral into something that messes with your mental. You've come a long way since your mom passed. I just want you to stay grounded."

"I know," I said, touched. "And that's why I love you. But I *have* to do this. I really believe something from my past is tied to why I connected with Alex and Imani the way I did. Imani especially. She never got tired of hearing about Mama—never rolled her eyes or changed the subject. She just... listened. Mama would've loved that about her."

"Poodah," Cynthia said gently, "I'm not trying to be harsh, but Imani *did* hurt you. Why do you think your mom would've still felt the same way after everything that happened? Maybe in the beginning, sure—but now?"

"I don't know. Maybe I'm reaching." I sighed, already second-guessing myself.

"Maybe just a little. But look," she leaned in, "I know you still love her. I can see it. And I've always respected how you live your life—unapologetically. You don't let people's opinions shake your foundation.

But this... this feels different. It's like you're trying to make sense of your past to make room for Imani again. And maybe that's okay. But if you miss her, just *say* that. I'm not here to judge you." Cynthia rubbed my arm, offering space to be honest.

"I just feel like I'm not *supposed* to want her back," I said quietly.

"You're human. That's all this is. You know I've got my own thoughts about Imani, but none of that matters. What matters is what *you* want."

"That's the problem—I don't know," I said, defeated.

"Damn. She really got you tangled up, huh?" Cynthia shook her head. "Whatever you decide, I've got your back. I mean, I like Kevin for you— he's solid. But your heart? It's still with Imani. I just don't want her to come back and hurt you all over again."

She was right. Kevin checked all the boxes. But Imani felt like... unfinished business. I wanted to know what she was up to. If she and Alex were done. If she was even capable of being emotionally present for me now. My thoughts were spinning.

"I hear you, Cynthia. And thank you—for always seeing me. Remember when you first met Imani? You gave her *the* look. Like, who is this chick and why does she know things I don't?"

"Girl, yes!" she laughed. "I was ready to throw hands. I was like, oh hell no, who does she think she is?"

"At the time we weren't even together like that. Just friends. I had no clue it was gonna turn into... all of *that.*"

"Mmhm. But I *knew.* Especially when you had that panic attack? The way she looked at you? Yeah. I clocked that real quick."

"Wait—you knew back then?" I asked, surprised.

"C'mon now. You remember I told you, 'That couple wants to fuck you?'"

"Oh my God, I *do* remember that!" I burst out laughing. "I thought you were just being messy."

"Girl, please. I know sexual tension when I see it. Being a call girl in college taught me a *lot.* I can read a room in three seconds flat."

"You're not wrong," I said, grinning. "Anyway, we should probably head out. The manager's been circling like a hawk. We've overstayed our welcome."

"And? She can use her words," Cynthia huffed, flipping through the menu like she was about to order dessert.

"Cynthia! The sign says two and a half hours for dine-in—we've been here three." I grabbed my purse and downed the last of my water.

"Ugh, fine. Come back to my place then. I'm free the rest of the day."

"Bet. You cool if I smoke?"

"Smoke what? A blunt? You're smoking again?"

"Yeah. I've been meaning to quit cold turkey, but during the pandemic? It helped me survive."

"Girl, I get it. No judgment here. I might even join you. Surprisingly, I haven't smoked once this whole pandemic."

"Really?"

"Yeah. Work wasn't too stressful once we went fully remote. And being at my mom's place was actually peaceful. I'm glad I moved her out the hood—otherwise I probably would've needed something stronger than weed," she chuckled.

"It's wild, right? What we've been able to do for our moms. I'm so glad mine got to see more of the world before she passed."

"We've really built beautiful lives," Cynthia said, getting serious for a moment. "We've traveled, we're healthy, we're doing what we love—and we have each other. Romantic drama aside, we've done alright. I love you, girl."

"I love you too." I smiled, my heart full.

"Aight, let's get out of here and blast off once we get to my place," she winked, checking her lipstick in her camera phone.

"Ha! I know *that's* right."

We walked out of the restaurant and hopped in an Uber back to her place. I couldn't stop thinking about how much Cynthia meant to me. She's been my constant since college—my ride or die. We've been through so much, and no matter what, she's never left my side. Friendships like ours deserve more love. Everyone talks about marriage, kids, and jobs like they're the only relationships that matter. But this? This friendship? It's held me together.

I don't know where things are headed—Kevin, Imani, Amanda—but one thing I *do* know? I'll figure it out. Probably after a few good hits of that blunt.

CHAPTER

4

This time a couple of years ago, I was in Bali for the Vitality Fest—and honestly, it was everything. Being the lead yoga instructor at a global wellness retreat? Dream come true. I'd been invited back the following year, but then the pandemic hit, and everything was canceled. This year, it's been postponed until fall, but my mind keeps drifting back.

Back to the people.

Back to the energy.

Back to Imani.

That trip? That's when I fell for her. I didn't know it at the time, but somewhere between the long talks, the effortless connection, and the soul-shaking sex, it happened. I fell in love with her under the Bali sun.

And now, sitting at my desk at work—supposed to be prepping for my last yoga class—I felt that pull again. That quiet ache in my chest. I couldn't help myself. I opened the Facebook app on my phone, telling myself it was just curiosity. Nothing more. It's been months—maybe even over a year—since I last saw or heard anything about Imani. Ever since I moved back to New York, I went cold turkey. No texts. No calls. No creeping. I needed her out of my system.

But clearly... I wasn't cured.

I typed in her name.

Nothing.

Weird.

I searched Instagram.

Still nothing.

Had she wiped herself off social media? Changed her name? My anxiety was creeping in. I tried not to overthink it. Maybe she just went low-key, or maybe she didn't want to be found.

Still, I wasn't ready to let it go. I typed in my brother's name—he used to be friends with a few of her people. I scrolled through his friends list until I spotted a tiny thumbnail photo. Wait. That looked like her. I tapped it.

Boom. There she was.

Short pixie cut. Confident stare. And her profile name now said *Imani Nicole.*

I blinked at the screen.

No more Alex's last name. That was code for "I'm single now." At least, that's how I read it.

My stomach flipped.

I kept scrolling. Post after post showed Imani with her daughter, Yaya—who was now a full-blown toddler, all curly brown hair and those same big eyes I used to get lost in. No Alex in sight. Just Imani, Yaya, and her mom. A new trio. A new chapter.

Then I saw it.

That picture.

A beach selfie. Skin glistening. That body? Snatched. Her abs were popping and her hips still curved in all the right ways. The caption read *#hotgirlsummer.*

I stared at the screen longer than I'd like to admit.

Why did she have to look that damn good? And where the *fuck* was Alex?

Another post from about a month ago caught my eye—something about the "new normal" of being a single mom. So it was true. She and Alex were done. Officially.

And now I was sitting here, trying to act like I didn't care. Trying to act like I wasn't wondering if she was dating someone new. If she still lived in Arizona. If she ever thought about *me*.

I looked back at her profile and stared at the "Add Friend" button. My finger hovered. I hesitated.

Class starts in five minutes.

I locked my phone. Told myself to focus.

But it was too late. My head was already flooded—with memories of us laughing, dancing, talking into the night, touching like we were the only two people on earth. I wanted that back. Even just a sliver of it. Just enough to remember what it felt like to be wanted like *that*.

Why did I even look her up?

Now I was spiraling. Now I wanted to *hear* her voice.

I unlocked my phone again, went back to her profile, and pressed "Add Friend."

There. It's done.

It's just a friend request, right?

No big deal.

Who the hell was I kidding?

I hope I'm not about to get myself into something I can't come back from.

"Hey, Serenity! I'm so excited for class tonight," Trisha said, snapping me out of my thoughts.

"Oh hey!" I replied, quickly masking my surprise. "You usually come on Mondays. It's good to see you here on a Wednesday too."

I forced a smile. That wasn't true—I kept track of my regulars, and Trisha was hard to miss. But I wasn't exactly thrilled to see her again. She'd been trying to turn yoga class into a budding friendship, and I just wasn't interested.

"Well, it's good to *be* seen," she said, exhaling dramatically as she peeled off her shoes and laid her mat down right behind where I normally stand. "My week has been a damn mess."

"I'm sorry to hear that," I said, already bracing myself.

"Thanks, girl. I've been having thyroid issues, the kids are driving me crazy, Chris is still drinking like he's in college, and honestly? I just needed to get the hell out of the house."

She launched into this saga while everyone else was still settling in, her voice loud and unfiltered like usual.

"You've definitely got a lot going on," I said, doing my best to sound encouraging.

"Hopefully class tonight will help. I'm looking forward to it too."

Students trickled in, and I caught a glimpse of someone through the glass.

Kevin.

He walked past my door, and my heart skipped. What was *he* doing here this late? That wasn't like him. I wanted to go ask, but class was starting in five minutes, and I prided myself on punctuality. Still, his presence now added another layer to the swirl of thoughts I couldn't seem to quiet—Imani, the friend request, and now, Kevin.

The class flew by in a blur. My body moved through the poses, but my mind wasn't really present. I was distracted and unsettled, not ready to face what I knew I needed to face.

Eventually, class wrapped, and students began rolling up their mats and heading out. All except Trisha, of course—she always lingered, moving slowly like her body was constantly at odds with her spirit. She wasn't even forty, but she carried herself like she was seventy. Limping, hunched, needy.

And always *oversharing*.

She once asked other students to carry her bags because her arms were sore. From what, exactly? Half the time she couldn't get through a full session without collapsing into child's pose for fifteen minutes. She had thyroid issues, sure—and she made damn sure everyone knew about it. That, and her kids, her husband, her drama. Not to mention the bags— what *was* in all those damn bags? And why the hell did she always have to be in everybody's business?

Kevin walked by again, and this time we locked eyes. He tapped on the door, silently asking if he could come in. I nodded and waved him in.

"Good evening, ladies. You all look amazingly rejuvenated," Kevin said with his signature smile.

Predictably, the women—including Trisha—perked up like groupies at a backstage door. Ponytails were adjusted, sweat was wiped, and one or two giggles escaped.

"Well, we're definitely rejuvenated now that *you're* here," Trisha called out, shameless.

"Aww, why thank you," he said, then turned to me. "Serenity, can I talk to you when you're done?"

"No worries. You can stay—class just ended," I said, returning his smile.

"Kevin, you should come to our classes more often," Trisha gushed, practically batting her lashes.

He chuckled politely. "I'm not here to spy on my instructors."

"Oh, you wouldn't be spying," she teased. "We'd *love* to have you."

I could feel my eye twitch. Was this woman really trying to flirt right now, with all that chaos she just confessed to twenty minutes ago?

"I appreciate that. I'll consider it next time," he said, humoring her. "Maybe I'll even join your class."

"Mmm hmm. You do that, sir." Trisha gave him a sly smile and swayed her way out of the room like she was walking a runway.

The door shut behind her and I let out a long sigh. "Oh my God. That woman is something else. I hate to be like this, but she *really* gets on my nerves."

Kevin laughed. "Yeah, she's... a lot. Figuratively *and* literally. But enough about her. I came to talk to *you*."

He closed the door, sealing us off from any more interruptions. I knew where this was going.

"Yes?" I asked, playing coy though my stomach was in knots.

"Serenity, what's up? I haven't really heard from you in a few days. I mean, yeah, we've texted the usual good mornings and sent a few memes... but I feel like something's off. I'm trying to figure out what's on your mind."

His voice was gentle but firm. And there it was—the moment I'd been avoiding.

"I just figured since you're pretty busy. I thought we'd catch up when you had time," I said, skimming over the truth. Imani was still on my mind like an itch I couldn't scratch, and I was itching to check Facebook to see if she'd accepted my request.

Kevin narrowed his eyes slightly. "So you're hitting me with the busy excuse, huh?" He smirked, but his tone was serious. "Just so you know, I'm *never* too busy for you. I only gave you space because I thought that's what you needed. But if you ever need me to do more to put your mind at ease, just say the word."

Damn. He was saying all the right things. Direct, intentional. Kevin wasn't playing games—he wanted me, and he was clear about it. But Imani... she was clouding my thoughts like a storm. I had no business still feeling something, but those photos, that smile, those memories—it all came rushing back and now I was tangled in the past.

Should I tell Kevin? No. Nothing had happened. It was just... curiosity. That's all.

"You're really an amazing man, you know that?" I reached for his hand, squeezing it gently.

"Aww, hell. Is this the part where you let me down easy?" Kevin's face shifted, a flicker of disappointment behind his playful expression.

"No. Not at all," I said quickly. "I'm not making any decisions right now. I just need some time. I've been through a lot and I want to take things slow."

He nodded, thoughtfully. "I respect that. You've always been open with me, and I appreciate that more than you know. How about this—let's go bowling and grab dinner sometime soon. No relationship talk, no pressure. Just fun."

That smile of his made it hard to say no. "Okay. I'm game."

"Alright then—it's a date," he said, a bit of hope in his voice.

"Great."

The silence that followed wasn't uncomfortable... just layered. I was distracted, honestly more interested in getting back to my phone than continuing the conversation, which made me feel like shit.

"Did you take an Uber here?" he asked.

"Yeah."

"My car's in the garage. I can give you a ride home if you want?"

It was tempting. God, it was tempting. I was already feeling a little flushed, but I knew better. Imani was the reason I was this wound up—not Kevin. If I gave in now, it'd only confuse things even more.

"Thank you, but I'm gonna lock up first and catch an Uber. I appreciate the offer though."

Kevin nodded, not pushing. "Just text me when you get home, alright? I want to make sure you're safe."

"I will. Thanks again." I leaned in and gave him a soft kiss on the cheek.

He caught my hand in his, kissed it slowly, then pulled me toward him. Time stalled. His hands found my waist and suddenly I was in his arms, his mouth on mine, the air thick with tension that had been building for weeks.

"Kevin—" I tried to speak between kisses. "I just finished teaching. I'm all sweaty."

He smiled against my lips. "And you think I give a damn?" he whispered, his voice low and rough. "That just makes you *real*. And even more irresistible."

My body responded before I could rationalize anything. He lifted me like I weighed nothing, revealing one of his tattoos—an ankh on his forearm that pressed against my skin as he held me. I wanted this. Maybe not forever, maybe not with clarity. But at that moment, I wanted to disappear into his touch.

Everything else—Imani, the past, the questions—faded for just a little while.

"Damn, Serenity... even after teaching class, you still taste incredible," Kevin whispered between kisses, his voice low and hungry.

He took his time, savoring me like I was his favorite dessert. Every slow, intentional movement sent ripples through my body, and I could feel my grip tighten around him—my thighs locked in pleasure I couldn't contain. Kevin always made love like it was an art form, his hands and mouth exploring me like he was rediscovering a hidden treasure.

"I thought you said we should wait... until I figured things out," I managed to gasp, caught in the haze of what he was doing to me.

He didn't answer with words. Instead, he kept going, determined and deliberate, until my body arched with release and I lost myself in the waves of sensation that washed over me.

Finally, when I opened my eyes, he looked up at me with a knowing grin.

"Now... what were you saying?" he asked, smug but sweet.

I shook my head, breathless. "You really are something else."

"I try," he said, pulling me closer.

I kissed him, deeply, tasting both of us and letting the moment blur the lines I'd tried so hard to define. One thing led to another—his clothes found the floor, and so did my better judgment. I welcomed him in every way, physically and emotionally, even if part of me wasn't sure if it was passion… or confusion… that I was responding to.

As we moved together, everything felt urgent, intense, and grounding all at once.

Maybe this was where I belonged. Maybe Kevin was the answer. Or maybe it was just the flood of oxytocin clouding the questions I hadn't answered yet.

CHAPTER

5

The scent of eucalyptus in the spa was absolutely divine. The massage, facial, manicure, and pedicure I'd just received were exactly what I needed. I almost didn't want to leave—I was floating from the pampering—but I'd promised myself a trip to the art gallery today.

As I approached the gallery, I couldn't help but bask in the beauty of this Sunday afternoon. The warmth of the sun, paired with the soft, sporadic breeze—something only the arrival of a new season could bring—was giving me life. I was on a mission to find a few new pieces to adorn my freshly painted walls. A student had recommended this particular gallery, and I was finally making time to explore it.

I'd started painting my home during the pandemic as a form of therapy. I still wasn't ready to open up to another therapist. Once you've had a Dr. Wilson in your life, it's hard to just sit and share your soul with anyone else.

So many times, I'd pause and ask myself, *"What would Dr. Wilson say?"* And honestly, that helped more than I expected. I'd spent so many hours in her chair that I could practically hear her voice in my head, guiding me through the emotional fog. Even now, she was still with me in spirit. Her presence—however intangible—was worth every dollar I'd ever spent.

The gallery was filled with vibrant, inspiring work. I felt like I'd walked into a treasure chest. My idea of "art" at home had usually been plants and namaste posters, but I'd recently been drawn to more contemporary and figurative pieces. Something bold. Something new. It felt good to shift my focus onto beauty and expression, instead of letting relationships and emotions dominate every corner of my mind.

Still, my thoughts wandered. Kevin lingered in my memory like a song I couldn't stop humming.

When we made love the other night—and yes, that was definitely love making—it felt… right. He touched me with such tenderness and intention. Not that he hadn't before, but in the past it was more primal, more driven by urgency. This time was different. He moved like he didn't want to let go. Like he was pouring something into me. And I felt it. Deeply. I love connecting with someone like that—when it's not just about the orgasm but the art of giving and receiving.

I kept debating whether to check Facebook to see if Imani had accepted my friend request. But I didn't want to ruin the high I was riding. If she hadn't, I'd be annoyed. If she had, I'd be consumed. I'd start obsessing, overthinking, reaching out. So I made the decision to just… not. Not yet. Maybe, if I waited long enough, I could let her go. Again.

But could I really move on with Kevin?

His new role as a father wasn't just his journey—it would become mine too. And Venise? Who's to say we'd even get along? If I'm in Kevin's life and around his daughter, Venise would naturally have a voice in that. I couldn't handle someone trying to tell me how to exist or love. What if Kevin took her side every time? What if he didn't have my back?

And what if his daughter didn't like me? What if every visit was a battlefield?

I wasn't trying to talk myself out of being with Kevin… but these were real questions. Important ones. Because the truth is—you never know how someone will respond until you're in the thick of it.

Yeah, Kevin was talking all that blissful stuff now—but what about later, as our relationship progressed? Was I even built for a life like that? I mean, I *might* just be too selfish at this stage of my life. Then again, he's not asking me to change everything… at least, I don't think he is. He just said he wants me to be his woman.

But what does that *really* look like?

For someone like me, I sure was doing a whole lot of worrying—and that's usually not my thing. Okay, maybe sometimes. Still, maybe I'll give this relationship with Kevin a shot. On one condition: **boundaries**. We'd need to set some major ground rules if this was going to work.

First, I want us to date for at least six months without me meeting his daughter. I need time to really feel this out and see if we both *want* this, not just crave each other.

Second, I need to get to know Kevin outside the bedroom. Clearly, we're sexually compatible—check. But how do we vibe when we're doing everyday things? Grocery shopping? Road tripping? Dealing with stress?

Third, I want to see how Kevin lives—*really* lives. I've been to his house. It's clean, organized, and smells nice. But he's also got a maid on payroll, so… that's not exactly the same as how he *manages life*. I want to know how he handles conflict, downtime, and how he balances his time— with himself and with me.

The older I get, the more I care about the specifics. These details matter. I'm not interested in playing house. I've been married before, and say what you want about Dave, but he set a certain standard. If I'm considering another committed relationship, certain things have to be in place.

To Kevin's credit, he's been completely transparent about Venise and his daughter, and I respect the hell out of that. I like when people can be honest with me, even when it's messy. That kind of vulnerability builds trust—the kind I want in my life all the time.

Still, my thoughts drifted.

Imani.

That level of intimacy and transparency we had? It never felt forced. It was effortless… until it wasn't. Reality came crashing in, but that didn't stop me from being completely captivated by her. Even now, every time I considered moving forward with Kevin, Imani popped back into my mind. Like a reflex.

The truth was, I was deeply attracted to both of them—for *very* different reasons. I'd been in a poly relationship before. Could that be an option again? But instead of Alex, it'd be Kevin and Imani. Now *that* was a fantasy.

Except—who was I kidding?

There's no telling if Imani is even still interested in me. And while the world might think two women is every man's dream, Kevin doesn't strike me as the type to be cool with a full-blown relationship triangle. Especially not one involving my *ex*.

Plus, he already knows too much about my history with Imani. That alone would make things awkward as hell. Still… the idea of being able to have *both*—a side of Kevin *and* Imani? Whew. That got me excited in a way that made me question *every* societal norm I'd ever learned.

Just as I was about to spiral into another daydream…

"Excuse me, miss. Can I help you find something? We have an amazing piece by an up-and-coming artist named Fletcher Simms. I think you might find his work really exciting."

The voice belonged to a slender red-haired woman with a wild, abstract fashion sense—like if a brushstroke came to life. She started describing the artist, and I instantly perked up. His work? Bold. Unapologetic. Fluid. It didn't follow rules—and I *loved* that. She nailed my taste like she knew me.

"You really hit the nail on the head with this one. This is *definitely* my style," I said, gawking at the piece she pointed out.

"Simms is one of my favorites," she gushed. "I've followed his work for a while, and mark my words—he's about to be *big*."

"Wow, I'd love this for my living room. How much?" I asked, already visualizing it above the fireplace.

"This one is going for $5,000. But trust me—when he blows up, pieces like this will start at $20,000."

I'd never spent more than $500 on a piece of art. But something about this felt right. This wasn't just about decorating. It was an investment in myself. In how I wanted to feel. In what I wanted to see every day in my home.

"Great, I'll take it!" I said, giddy like I'd just scored an iconic piece off an episode of *The Cosby Show*.

"Perfect. I'll get that wrapped up and ready for checkout. Oh! I can't believe I forgot—Fletcher Simms will actually be *here* at the gallery the

Saturday after next. He's debuting some new work. You should definitely come!"

"That sounds amazing. I'll lock it into my calendar. Thanks so much for the heads up!"

As she walked away, my eyes returned to the art piece—and in that moment, I didn't think about Kevin, or Imani, or anyone else.

It was just me.

Choosing something beautiful.

"Most definitely! Here are a few flyers. Be sure to spread the word. We're really trying to put ourselves on the map when it comes to bringing in fresh talent. We're all about educating people on quality art—and introducing patrons to hidden gems."

"Wow, thank you. And yes, I'll definitely spread the word!"

I felt like such a grown-up buying my first *real* piece of art—and attending a major event featuring an up-and-coming artist. I couldn't help but think about how much Imani would love something like this. She always had an eye for things that moved the soul.

It reminded me of how Dave used to get whenever he attended tech conferences or came back from networking with other Silicon Valley types—excited, buzzing. He'd drop $10,000 or $20,000 without blinking on some cutting-edge gadget or software for the house or one of his ventures. That was his thing. And I'm starting to get it now—how exhilarating it is to discover a world you didn't even know you'd love.

Art was doing that for me.

I wanted to immerse myself in it—especially fine art. Paintings, in particular. I'm surprised I never tapped into this before, but hey—timing is everything. And honestly, before marrying Dave, this kind of lifestyle just wasn't financially accessible to me.

And I'll always be grateful for marrying him—not just because of the money, but because he really did open up another world to me. A world I may not have otherwise known existed. When we first split, there were times I wondered if we'd made a mistake. But then I'd remind myself—*he* was the one who wanted the divorce.

Could I have tried to convince him to stay? Maybe. But I was drowning in grief. And it didn't feel like my job to fight for something I wasn't sure I even wanted anymore.

Looking back, even if we *had* stayed together, I think we would've grown apart eventually. We had some beautiful times, sure. But I would've fallen out of love with Dave. We just… vibe better as friends now. There's no romantic spark anymore.

I think what always stuck with me was how *distracted* our marriage felt. Always people at the house, always out with groups. Rarely just the two of us. Sexually, there was no heat left. And honestly, I didn't mind when he traveled because I loved being alone. Over time, I stopped picturing a future with him.

Sometimes I wonder if he started to feel the same way—because leaving me right after Mama died? That was brutal. I mean, he *did* stay around for a bit to help with the yoga classes, and he tried to coax me out of bed each day. But I guess there's only so much a person can take when the love is fading.

In therapy with Dr. Wilson, I focused so much on grief that I never really explored the divorce itself. At the time, I didn't see the point—he initiated it, after all. What was there to analyze?

But now, after everything I've lived through… I'm wondering if revisiting my divorce might actually help me decide what I want with Kevin. And even Imani.

"Miss…"

The gallery assistant gently interrupted my spiral of thoughts.

"Oh! You can call me Serenity," I replied with a smile.

"I'm so sorry, Serenity—you looked deep in thought. I just wanted to let you know that I've got the Simms piece wrapped and ready. I can check you out over here."

"Okay, great! Thank you again so much for your help. I can't explain it, but I'm really excited to learn more about art and find pieces that speak to me—and to my home."

"If you're interested," she said, lowering her voice conspiratorially, "our gallery works with some incredible home curators. They often source pieces directly from us for their clients. I'd be happy to connect you?"

"Oh my God, that would be amazing!"

Wow. I was *really* getting into this art stuff.

Wait until I tell Cynthia what I've been up to.

*****

"Girl, I know I say this all the time, but I'm *so* happy you're living in New York again," Cynthia said, sipping her wine as we lounged on my couch, feet kicked up on my custom bamboo ottoman.

"And you can keep saying it," I laughed.

"There you go. Aren't you glad to be back here with *me* too?" she asked, her voice playful like a school kid fishing for a gold star.

"Of course, honey. You know I'm just messing with you. This move—this whole chapter—has been one of the best decisions I've ever made. You know how I am: I don't repeat things and I don't look back. Once I left New York, I didn't think I'd return—same way I didn't go back to Dave. When I move on, I move *on*. But coming back now, at this stage in my life? It feels right. And with how much the city's changed, it's like I moved somewhere new anyway."

"You're not wrong," Cynthia nodded. "And you *definitely* don't look back—that's facts. So… you know I gotta ask. Does this mean Imani is a no-go?"

She raised her eyebrows like she was daring me to contradict myself.

"That's the million-dollar question, isn't it?" I sighed. "I still haven't checked Facebook to see if she accepted my friend request. I just… haven't brought myself to look. But as far as going back? Damn. It's hard to say. Now that she's divorced, things *could* be different…"

"Are you asking me? Or trying to convince yourself?" Cynthia tilted her head. "'Cause my thought is: leave the bitch alone." She took another sip of wine and smirked.

"Well damn. Tell me how you *really* feel," I said, half-laughing, half-salty.

"I'm just calling it like I see it. She's cool and all, but she hurt you, *Poodah,* and I can't go for that. You're not still hooked on the cat like that, are you?"

I gave her a sly look. "Well… that part *was* good."

"Uugh! Girl, spare me. I've kissed a few girls in my day, but putting my face in another woman's cooch is where I absolutely draw the line."

"Don't knock it till you try it."

"How about *no*. I ain't gotta try it to know I'm good." Cynthia waved me off. "But seriously—Imani had you seeing stars, yeah, but let's not forget *Kevin*. That man has it together. Yeah, he just found out he's got a daughter, but he's been straight-up with you from the jump. He wants *you*, just you. He doesn't seem confused. At all. So if you must get a few more rounds in with Imani, do your thing—but don't you dare start a relationship back up with her."

"I guess you're right," I said with a shrug.

"Don't 'guess' me. Don't do it for *me*. Do it for you. Kevin deserves someone who's all in. So if you're not, don't leave that man hanging."

"But *that's* the thing, Cynthia. I *am* into him. Deeply. But this daughter thing—it threw me for a loop."

"I know it did. But is it a dealbreaker? Like, *really*? 'Cause Imani got a whole toddler herself and that ain't stopping you from wanting to crawl back into her bed. I'm just saying."

Cynthia had a point.

What *was* really stopping me from moving forward with Kevin? We had such a natural vibe. We enjoyed each other's company. He made me laugh. He made me feel seen. But still—Imani being unattached now, newly divorced, it complicated things.

Not that I even knew what she was up to anymore.

Hell, for all I know, she might not even want to talk to me.

"Damn, Cynthia. I'm legit confused. And I *hate* being confused. I like knowing what I'm doing, and just *doing* it."

The wine had started to hit. And maybe it *was* the alcohol, or maybe it was something deeper, but all I could think about was *Imani*. Finding her. Touching her. Making love to her.

"I know, babe," Cynthia said gently. "And that's why I'm here. I *know* you don't want the traditional kids-marriage-minivan setup. You've always walked your own path. But have you thought about talking to Kevin? Like really laying it out—telling him you want him in your life, but that you want Imani to be part of it too?"

"Girl… *hell* no," I said, eyebrows raised.

"Why not? I mean, Kevin strikes me as pretty progressive. Open-minded."

"I don't think it's about that. I think he might be down for a threesome here or there, but I doubt he wants Imani sitting at our dinner table on Sundays."

"Fair. You got a point." Cynthia smirked. "You'll figure it out."

She leaned back and stretched.

"Now, not to change the subject—but what you got to eat up in this house?"

"I think I've got some leftover—"

"Wait a minute. *Leftovers?*" She stopped me mid-sentence. "No, boo. Let's just order some food and put on a movie or something."

We cracked up, ordered from Uber Eats, and settled in for one of our favorite lazy girl nights.

But halfway through the movie, the doorbell rang.

Cynthia and I looked at each other, wide-eyed, silently asking the same thing:

Who the hell could that be?

"Girl, why you looking at me like that? This *yo'* house. Go get the door," Cynthia laughed, barely lifting her glass.

"I *know* it's my house. I just wasn't expecting anybody—especially not after the food already came."

I got up slowly, still staring toward the front as I walked. I peeked through the side window—it was a delivery guy.

"Yes? Who is it?" I asked, firm and cautious through the door. Living alone in New York teaches you to never open the door blindly.

"Yes ma'am, I have a delivery for Serenity Hayes," he responded.

I glanced back at Cynthia and gave her *the look*—our old college signal we'd use whenever something felt... off. She clocked it instantly.

I cracked the door open slowly, only to be greeted by a *massive* bouquet of white calla lilies—my absolute favorite—and a small, square gift box.

"Are you Serenity Hayes?" he asked.

"Yes, I'm Serenity."

"I just need your signature here."

"Umm... okay?" I signed the receipt, still confused. I hadn't ordered anything.

"Thanks, ma'am. Have a great evening." He gave a polite nod and walked off.

I stepped back inside, clutching the box in one hand and the bouquet in the other.

"*Wooooow*, Poodah… who's that from?" Cynthia asked, eyes wide, already halfway invested.

"Girl, I have *no* idea, but I'm about to find out." I set the bouquet down on the entry table, scanning for a note. Nothing. Then I flipped the box over, looking for a return address.

The only thing listed was "African Accents."

"Ever heard of a place called African Accents?" I asked, raising an eyebrow.

Cynthia shook her head. "Nope."

I opened the box—and there it was. The most *stunning* ankh necklace I'd ever seen. Elegant. Weighty. Ancient yet modern. It looked almost exactly like Kevin's tattoo.

And then I saw the note.

"Oh my God… girl. It's from *Kevin*! I have to read this to you."

I unfolded the card and read it aloud, my voice catching as I went:

I'm gonna go deep for a moment, so just bear with me. I bought you this ankh necklace—and hopefully the calla lilies arrived at the same time—because both symbolize life. And honestly, that's what you breathed back into me when we met. My business is thriving, I'm living good, and I'm blessed with amazing family and friends. But Serenity, you've been the key ingredient I didn't know I was missing. I want to explore so much more with you.

You once told me how much you loved my ankh tattoo, so I thought you might like this. And I know you're a plant girl, so I figured the calla lilies would speak to your spirit. I just wanted to give you a little something to let you know how much you mean to me. Am I trying to win you over? Hell yeah. But I swear—this is genuine. This is from my heart.

"*Biiiiiitttccchhhh*," Cynthia whispered, stunned.

"Wow," I said softly, holding the card to my chest. "That was… beautiful."

Cynthia set her wine down and gave me the *most* dramatic look.

"Now listen. Do we *really* have to think about this anymore? He's fine, successful, rich as hell, loves his mama, willing to step up for a kid he just found out about, and now he's sending you stuff like *this?*" She pointed at the flowers like they were evidence in court.

"Honey, this is a *no-brainer,*" she said, staring at me like:

Girl. Just go be with him already.

6

I was pretty excited about going to the art gallery tonight for the Fletcher Simms Meet and Greet. I really wished Cynthia could've come, but she had to work late—and Kevin was swamped, too.

Speaking of Kevin… after that gift he sent me? Let's just say we had our own little *reconnecting* session. But honestly, I can't even reduce it to just *having sex*. Our souls merged on some next-level type of intimacy. The way he held me, looked at me, caressed me—and then just *laid* with me afterward—it was electric. I wish I could bottle that experience up and carry it with me wherever I go.

We ended up talking a lot, too. About ourselves. About what this relationship could be. I still didn't confirm anything official between us, but every day, I find myself leaning closer to him. Still… I'd be lying if I said I wasn't nervous about him being a newfound parent. That just wasn't in my original picture. I'm sure his daughter is lovely, but I also know they need real time to get to know each other. I don't want to interfere with that—and I *damn sure* don't want to feel like I'm competing for his attention. Kevin says I'm a priority, and while I want to believe that, I guess only time will tell.

Anyway, do I want to go dressy or casual tonight? I've never been to an art gallery event like this before. Maybe I'll land somewhere in the middle. I know people will be snapping pictures, and if I end up in one, I want to at least look halfway decent. Fletcher Simms definitely has a following—the contemporary art group I'm in on Facebook has been blowing up with posts about tonight's event. It'll be nice to finally meet some of these folks in person.

I settled on a cute sundress and strappy sandals, letting my hair be free and full in its natural curls. I kept my makeup light and fresh-faced, with a soft summer scent you'd only catch if the wind hit just right. I wanted to look like I belonged there—even if this wasn't really my usual scene. I grabbed an Uber, of course—because hardly anybody drives in New York.

When I arrived, the line outside was surprisingly long. I didn't mind, though. People-watching kept me entertained. The crowd was a whole *mood*—eclectic, artistic, vibrant. All kinds of people had shown up to support this up-and-coming artist. It reminded me of the first time I saw Jill Scott in North Philly, right before *Who Is Jill Scott?* dropped. None of us knew she was about to become *that* girl. Who knows—maybe one day I'll say I remember Fletcher Simms from the beginning.

Inside the gallery, people were mingling with friends, smiling, sipping drinks, and discussing the artwork. I kind of wished I had someone to hang with too, but honestly, being alone meant I could really focus. If Cynthia were here, she'd have me doubled over laughing. And if Kevin were here? He'd be trying to grab my ass every five minutes—and we'd probably end up sneaking off into a bathroom somewhere to *handle things*. So, maybe this was for the best.

I grabbed my complimentary drink and started strolling through the exhibits. The work was stunning—bold, emotional, vivid. Before Fletcher's introduction, I figured I'd run to the bathroom quickly so I wouldn't miss anything.

As I got closer to the hallway, I noticed a woman from behind who had a silhouette that looked *a lot* like Imani. Wishful thinking, I figured. But then—her voice. That voice. It was *identical.* My heart skipped. She had the same pixie cut as in her profile pic.

Could that *really* be her? Here? In *New York?*

I hadn't seen Imani since before the pandemic—since *before* I moved back. We hadn't spoken. Hell, I couldn't even bring myself to check if she'd accepted my Facebook friend request.

Then she turned around.

And it was her.

We locked eyes. And in that one moment, every memory came rushing back—good, bad, *everything.* She was still so damn beautiful. A new tattoo wrapped around her outer calf. Her body was fit, her presence bold. There was something about her now—more rooted. More assured. Like she was fully embracing whoever she had become.

We began walking toward each other, slowly, unsure of whether a hug was even appropriate. But we hugged anyway.

And *damn.* Her embrace was everything. Her skin was soft, her scent magnetic. I wanted to grab her ass so bad—but this wasn't 2018, and I needed to snap out of it.

"Wow… Imani. You look amazing," I said—sounding like a thirsty ass teenager.

"You do too. I thought I saw you in line earlier but I wasn't sure," she said, lightly rubbing my arm. *Lawd,* I was still weak for this woman.

"This is a pleasant surprise. I didn't expect to see you here in New York," I said, fishing gently.

"I'll be honest," she said, voice calm but sincere, "I'm surprised you're even happy to see me. I know we didn't end on the best note… and I know I played a big part in that. I just want to say I'm sorry. Again."

Her voice cracked slightly. But her eyes didn't waver.

"You don't have to apologize. That was a while ago. I'm not holding any grudges." I paused, then—*ugh,* why did I say it—"I even sent you a friend request on Facebook."

Damn. Why'd I let that slip? Now I *really* sound thirsty.

"Oh, seriously? I'm sorry about that," Imani said, her tone softening. "I don't really check my socials much anymore. When Alex and I separated— and eventually divorced—it just became too much. Seeing all the 'happy' couples, the curated love stories… I couldn't take it. And I definitely didn't want to deal with people asking questions."

There was hurt in her voice. Maybe even shame.

"I'm sorry to hear about you and Alex," I said automatically. Truthfully? I wasn't sorry at all.

"No, it was for the best. We were on completely different pages. I caught him cheating." She shrugged like it barely fazed her now. "Honestly? I probably deserved it with the way I handled things between us."

"Imani, come on," I said firmly. "At the end of the day, *he* made that decision. That's on him."

I stopped myself from blurting out that I'd seen him and Melissa together—back before I moved to New York. That wasn't my truth to drop, not tonight.

"Yeah," she said with a distant exhale, "but enough about him. What about you? What's been going on since you moved out here?"

She sounded genuinely curious—but also like she was gently steering the conversation away from her own regrets.

"Whew… a lot," I said, chuckling softly. "Too much to cover right here, honestly. How long are you in New York? Maybe we can talk about it over lunch—or dinner?"

I could've summed up my life in five minutes. But I wanted more time with her. Alone time.

"I'm here for a couple more days," she said, her voice a little mysterious.

"Okay, cool." I tilted my head, studying her. "So, is it okay if I ask what brought you to New York?" Because like—*really?* After all this time, how did she just happen to be here?

Imani looked at me for a beat. Then she took a deep breath.

"Serenity, I'm just gonna be straight with you. I wasn't totally honest earlier."

My stomach clenched, just a little.

"After Alex and I split," she continued, "I went back to singing. Started booking a few local gigs back home. One of my girls has a show in Brooklyn tomorrow night, so I came to support her—and network a little. That part's true."

She hesitated, then added, "The part I left out… I was invited to this Facebook art group a while ago. I didn't plan on joining, but I got curious. I started scrolling through the member list and I saw *you*. When I clicked on your profile, I noticed your friend request. I didn't know if I wanted to accept it just yet. But then I saw you were planning to come to this event tonight…"

She looked at me carefully.

"I figured, since I'd already be in New York, maybe I'd come. Just to see if I might run into you."

There it was. A confession wrapped in hesitation. Her eyes searched mine like she wasn't sure how I'd take it.

I didn't know how to feel, either.

"So… you wanted to know what I was up to," I said slowly, "but weren't sure how you felt about *me.*"

She nodded, eyes a little watery now. "Think about how things ended," she said quietly. "You had every right to be upset with me. I felt that. I *still* feel it sometimes."

Her lips were trembling slightly. Her vulnerability was catching me off guard.

I swallowed. "Are you here alone? Or… are you here *with* someone?"

If I was about to get dragged back into Imani's world, I needed to know what I was walking into.

"I mean," she said carefully, "I'm *here* with someone—but not *with* someone."

I narrowed my eyes. "Sooo… what does that mean?"

She gave me a sheepish smile. "One of the singers I rock with is here. We've messed around before, but we're not in a relationship. She's over at another exhibit talking to someone else. It's not like that. I promise."

It sounded like she meant it. But who was I to even question her? It had been years.

"Well," I said, letting my voice soften, "I'm pretty sure they're going to be introducing Fletcher soon. Maybe we can grab something to eat afterward? Just talk. No pressure."

Imani looked at me again—and this time, her gaze held something heavy. Something hopeful.

"Honestly, Serenity… I'd love that."

We locked eyes. The air between us tightened.

And all I could think was: *Oh, shit.*

*****

Imani said she had a taste for Mediterranean food, so I took her to one of my favorite spots in Downtown Brooklyn. The ambiance was everything—dim lighting, impossibly high ceilings draped with flowing white curtains, and Greek pop music humming in the background. It was a whole *vibe.*

We were a vibe.

Across the table, I couldn't take my eyes off her—ripped jean shorts, an off-the-shoulder top that hinted just enough, minimal makeup, and that confident little pixie cut. She looked effortlessly hot. Not trying too hard. Just *being.* There was a lightness about her—like she was finally breathing freely in her own skin.

And then there was her scent—lemongrass with a trace of something deeper... sandalwood, maybe. Subtle. Clean. Hypnotic.

Back in the day, we wouldn't have made it through appetizers without sneaking off somewhere to tear into each other. And honestly? I could feel the heat between us simmering just below the surface. But tonight felt different. We were playing it safe. Or at least, I was. My heart wasn't in the mood to be reckless again. And I wasn't sure where she stood.

"I'm so excited to hear you're singing again," I said, trying to steady my voice. "That's amazing."

"Who you telling?" Imani grinned. "It's been a long time coming. I should've done it sooner. Honestly, though, I don't think I'll be in Scottsdale much longer. There's just... not much for me there anymore, not with the direction I want to go."

I leaned in, intrigued.

"The only reason I'm there now is for Yaya. Alex wanted to stay close to her, so I stayed put—for a while. But lately, I've been thinking about heading back to Atlanta. I need to be around *my* people. My family. Scottsdale served its purpose, but I think I outgrew it the moment Alex and I split."

"Oh wow. Atlanta?" I echoed, arching a brow.

"What?" she asked, suddenly looking self-conscious. "You don't think that's the move?"

"No, no—it's not that. I just... I thought you said after college you never wanted to move back. You seemed so *adamant.*"

She laughed softly, a little embarrassed. "Yeah, well. That was college Imani—head over heels, ride-or-die, would've followed Alex to *Canada* if he asked." She rolled her eyes. "I'm not that girl anymore."

"I can tell," I said, smirking a little as I sipped my water.

She narrowed her eyes playfully. "Okay, what's that look for?"

"I'm just saying… you seem different. Like you know who you are now. What you want. *For you*. It's… alluring, honestly."

Imani bit her lip slightly, then smiled. "You're not wrong. I know it sounds cliché, but I'm finally doing *me*. Not shrinking. Not orbiting someone else's sun."

She glanced down at her hands for a second, then met my eyes again—clear, vulnerable.

"I'm done being anybody's plus-one. I want to be the *main event*, you know?"

"It makes perfect sense." And it did. Because the woman sitting across from me—the one radiating this calm fire—was the same woman I fell in love with back then. I *saw* her even when she couldn't see herself. But now? Now she wasn't hiding.

"I've talked enough," Imani said, tilting her head. "What about you? Still at the yoga studio? Anyone… special in your life?"

There it was. *That* question.

I believed in transparency—but something about talking about Kevin just didn't feel right. Maybe because I didn't even know where things stood with him. Or maybe because, right now, it felt like *this—Imani and me*—was the only thing that mattered.

"Well," I began, choosing my words carefully, "I'm still at the studio. It's a beautiful space—really grounding. Going from owning my own business to working for someone again was an adjustment, but I've got a lot of autonomy, which helps."

I paused, my tone softening. "Unfortunately, Dr. Wilson passed away during the thick of the pandemic."

Imani's face fell. "Oh no… I'm so sorry, Serenity."

"Thank you," I said gently. "She meant a lot to me. Losing her was… hard. It shook a lot loose."

We were quiet for a moment. Not awkward—just still. Present.

Imani reached across the table and lightly grazed my hand. Her touch was feather-light, but it sent a current up my arm. She didn't pull away right away, and neither did I.

There was so much more I wanted to say.

But for now, I just let the silence speak.

"Again, I'm truly sorry about Dr. Wilson." Imani's fingers closed around mine, this time with a weight that told me she meant every word.

"Yeah, that fucking sucked, I won't lie. I was asked to speak at her funeral. I mean, yes—she had dementia, but she still felt *so* vibrant, you know?" I paused, letting the memory settle. "We only occupy this space for a period of time. We all have an expiration date. But she was a huge part of my life—helped me get through some dark-ass moments. All the more reason to truly live life on your own terms."

I looked at Imani, searching her face for agreement.

"You're absolutely right. And that's something I really learned from *you*. I'm trying to do more of that now myself," she said, then softened. "But again, I know that must've been so hard. Did you go through that alone? Did you have anyone there for you?"

Her question was tender but also loaded—she wanted to know if someone else had filled her spot.

"Well, you know Cynthia's here in New York, so she was around. She did spend a lot of time in Baltimore with her mom during the pandemic, but she always checked in. As far as anyone else..." I shrugged. "An occasional hook-up here and there. Nothing serious."

I didn't lie. Kevin and I had our moments, but it wasn't anything real. Not yet, anyway.

"Understood. I'm glad you had Cynthia. She'd drop anything for you, and I know that." She paused. "So since you've been out here, it's just been hook-ups? Nothing promising?"

Imani was definitely fishing now—and it was kind of cute.

"Are you trying to see if someone's captured my heart since we broke up?" I asked, smirking.

"You *know* that's where I'm going with this," she said, laughing.

"All you had to do was say that."

Our waitress came by to take our order. I was unusually indecisive, while Imani seemed more eager to get back to our *real* conversation than to pick an entrée. Once she left, she slid in a little closer.

"So, you were saying…" she grinned, her eyes daring me to escape.

"It's like this, Imani. There *is* someone in my life right now. He wants more, and I'm not sure I do."

I took a sip of my drink and let the words hang.

"You said *he.*"

"Right. That surprise you?" I asked.

"Hmm… I guess not. I know you like men *and* women, but I always felt like women were more your speed," she said, leaning in like she knew me better than I knew myself.

"Well, you know better than to box me in. I like who I like."

"But do you still like *me?*" Imani locked eyes with me. No hesitation. No filter.

"Of course I still like you. Hell, I still love you. That hasn't changed."

"Damn it, Serenity. Then why are we still sitting here? We know what we both want. Why are we pretending?"

I couldn't help but smile. "So someone's gotten a little more assertive, huh?"

"I'm just saying." She looked serious now. "One thing my divorce taught me is that I'm done tiptoeing around what I want. And *right now?* I want *you.* I want to feel you. I want to hear you moan. I want your hands on me in all the right places. And honestly, I don't care about food unless I'm eating *you.*"

Her voice was steady, low, and dead ass serious—and it turned me *all* the way on.

"Damn… you're on your shit tonight," I breathed. "Not gonna lie, it's throwing me a little."

"So again, why are we still *sitting* here?" she said, slipping her hand under the table. She slid it up my thigh, her fingers finding my panties, brushing over my clit like she had every right to still know me like this.

"This might come as a shock," I said, trying to catch my breath, "but as much as I'd love to take you back to my place and *fuck the entire shit out of you* right now, it can't go down like this."

"You *can't* be serious," Imani said, grabbing my chair leg and pulling it closer. "Like you said, I'm on one tonight. I'm only here for a couple more days, I'm horny as hell, and I'm trying to *get into this.*"

I took a breath. "Imani… I get it. I really do. And trust me, I feel it too. But you're high, and I can tell right now you're craving a *good time.* You know I can give you that. But I've got some shit to sort through. It's been a minute."

I looked her in the eyes, serious now. "I'm happy for you. I am. You're glowing, you're alive, you're free. But I need to know where your *head* is at, not just where your hands are."

She paused for a moment, then gave me that signature smirk. "Yeah… speaking of head—"

Our waitress returned just in time with our food.

"Can I get you two ladies anything else?" she asked, sweetly oblivious.

"You most certainly can… the check," Imani said, never breaking eye contact with me.

CHAPTER

7

I was awakened by the chirping of birds and the blinding sun streaming through my bedroom window. Then came the unmistakable scent of something delicious cooking. I slowly made my way downstairs, each step revealing more clothing strewn across the floor—a trail of passion from the night before. That's when it all came back to me.

The wild night Imani and I had.

As I turned the corner into the kitchen, I saw her—gorgeous, glowing, wearing one of my old oversized yoga t-shirts. She was making coffee, dancing, and singing along to something in her AirPods like this was just another Sunday morning in our shared life.

"Imani!" I said, raising my voice slightly so she could hear me.

She turned, smiling. "Oh hey, hun. I didn't want to wake you—you were sleeping so good. I figured I'd start on breakfast. Want some coffee?"

Her tone was casual, soft. Like this was routine. Like she'd never left.

"Umm… sure?" I replied, still half-confused, half-enchanted.

"You good?" she asked, pouring a mug like this was *her* kitchen too.

"I mean, I'm okay. You?"

"I'm *wonderful.* Last night was the *shit.*" She beamed, like she was still riding the wave.

She glided toward me, kissed me softly, and I couldn't help but notice how the cut-off sleeves of my shirt exposed her side boobs. She looked edible.

"Yeah, I can tell. You're definitely in a good mood."

"Well, we've never had any issues in the bedroom. Or the bathroom. Or the kitchen. Hell, even the stairs." She winked, took a slow sip of her coffee, and passed me a steaming cup of my own.

"So Imani… listen—"

"Shhh…" she whispered, placing her finger on my lips. She set her mug down, took mine from my hand, and placed it on the sink. Then she reached for my hand, guiding it beneath the hem of the shirt she'd affectionately claimed as her own—straight between her legs. No panties. Nothing but warmth and wetness.

Imani was on *a mission,* and clearly didn't give a fuck. She guided my fingers exactly where she wanted them, moaning softly as I took over. Her breath quickened, her body swaying, her whispers turning into pleas—*don't stop.* The sound of her, the feel of her, how responsive her body was—it had me spiraling too.

I grabbed her waist, lifted her onto the counter, coffee be damned. A mug spilled and shattered in the background but neither of us noticed. She spread her legs wide, inviting me in with that look. I went down on her like it was communion, and the way her body responded let me know she'd been craving this as much as I had. Her thighs clamped around me so tight I almost couldn't breathe. But I didn't stop. I wanted her to feel everything.

And she did.

Afterward, we collapsed in the living room, naked, tangled up, her voice now singing directly to me. Her fingers trailed through my messy hair, and that smile—God, I missed that smile. If I could capture that moment and frame it, I would've.

But even in the quiet aftermath, the questions started to creep in.

"Babe… what are we doing?" I asked softly.

Imani chuckled. "Umm… pretty sure we're enjoying each other's company to the *fullest.*"

"You're not wrong," I smiled. "But seriously. What is this? Are we just picking up where we left off?"

I needed clarity. I needed *truth*. And I needed to figure out what I was going to do about Kevin.

Imani looked at me, gently. "I know you want to figure this out. But if I'm being completely honest… I don't know. We ran into each other and let things unfold the way they were supposed to."

"Well, not *exactly*," I teased. "You kind of knew I'd be at that art gallery."

She laughed, caught. "Okay, yeah. I had a little intel."

We both fell into that space—where old love mixes with new energy, where comfort collides with confusion. It was intoxicating. It was dangerous. And it was real.

Imani sat up, giving me a look I couldn't quite read. "So basically, you're saying I plotted all this. And even if I *did*… are you mad about it?"

"No. Not at all. That's why I'm asking—what are we doing, Imani? We haven't seen or spoken to each other in years. We didn't exactly end on the best note. You know how I felt about you, and then—bam—you show up. You're divorced, you're talking about moving to Atlanta. So… was this just sex?"

I felt myself opening up more than I wanted to. Being vulnerable with Imani felt like a risky game.

Imani looked at me, calm but serious. "Babe… I hadn't really thought about all that yet. We just saw each other last night. I haven't figured out the details of *us*. I mean, we both live in different states, and we've got full lives. I'm not asking you to change your whole game plan for me. That wouldn't be fair."

"Just like it wasn't fair when you lied to Alex the whole time you and I were together?" My voice cracked with the words. The hurt I buried long ago came rushing up.

Imani's face dropped. "Whoa. I mean, it wouldn't be fair to act shocked that stuff from the past is coming up. But you're really coming for me right now."

She stood and pulled a blanket from the couch, wrapping it around her.

"Listen, I'm sorry. I just… I wasn't expecting this. I wasn't expecting *you*. I've been fine not stressing about relationships, but with you—it's always been different. It took me forever to let go of us. And now you're here, in the flesh, and my mind won't stop racing. I'm scared of setting myself up again. I can't believe it's hitting me this hard."

Imani softened. "Can we just enjoy this moment? Catch up, see where things go, without putting pressure on it?"

"So it's just…" I paused.

"What's the problem?" she asked, scooting next to me and throwing the blanket over us both.

"I've been kind of… seeing someone."

Imani tilted her head, unfazed. "Mmhmm. You told me that last night. I've been dating too."

"But… he wants something serious."

I watched her face, searching for any flicker of discomfort—something to tell me she still wanted *me*.

Imani nodded. "Sounds like something you might want to explore. So… are you in love?"

"I… like him. A lot." I looked down, fidgeting with my hands.

"That's not what I asked." She raised an eyebrow. "Let me try again: do you see a *future* with this man?"

"I thought I did. Until you showed up." I exhaled. "I haven't forgotten about you, Imani. But I've been lowkey waiting for some kind of sign to just *move on* with him. He's got everything going for him. But he just found out he has a daughter… and I don't know if I want that kind of priority right now."

Imani tilted her head, amused. "You *do* realize I have a daughter, right? And you bonded with her *really* well in Arizona. So what's actually holding you back from moving forward with this guy? Because it doesn't sound like it's about the kid."

She gently took my hand, noticing how anxious I was. She always knew how to calm me.

"See, *this—you—*are what's holding me back," I admitted. "You just… *know* me. Even after two years, you still say all the right things. Kevin is amazing, truly. But with you, I feel like I'm home. I don't know if I'm just stuck on the familiarity of us, but I *want* this. Dammit, I said it. I want *you.*"

I could feel my eyes welling up, and I hated that.

Imani inhaled deeply. "Serenity… I'm trying to tie up some loose ends in my life. Things with Alex are still messy, and I know he's going to lose it when I tell him I'm planning to move. He won't want to be far from Yaya. And honestly, my music career is finally gaining traction. I'm happy. I still want you in my life, but maybe not in the way you're hoping. I've missed you too. But I've done a lot of healing. I've been learning how to move forward."

"So basically, I dumped you, and you've learned to live without me—and now you're not going back," I said bitterly.

Imani looked at me, carefully. "What's interesting is… you've always been the free spirit. Chill about relationships but sure of what you want. But *this*—this version of you? I've never seen you quite like this. You were always vulnerable before, but now… you're baring your *soul.* And honestly, it's turning me on."

She leaned in, kissing my neck, and I started melting into her again. But then the questions crept back in. I gently nudged her away.

"But again—where does that leave us?" My voice was low but firm.

Imani looked at me squarely. "You want the truth? I've always wanted you, Serenity. But the timing? It's not right. I'm not ready to shift my life just to see if this might work. I'd *love* to stay connected—see each other, hang out, catch up…"

"Right. And fuck," I said, my voice sharp.

"Damn, babe," she snapped. "When did you become such a fucking prude? What happened to the free-spirited Serenity I used to know?"

She stood and started picking her clothes off the floor.

"Oh, so now that you're not married anymore, you just wanna fuck your way through your freedom? That it?"

I knew I was spiraling, but I couldn't stop. I was so *in love* with her—and terrified of losing her all over again. I thought maybe… this was fate. That we ran into each other for a *reason.* But clearly, I was wrong.

Imani turned, fire in her eyes. "You've got a lot of nerve talking to me like this. I've been honest with you—no games, no bullshit. *Total* transparency. And this is how you respond? It's not like I'm counting us out. I'm saying I need *space* to figure out my shit. But you—you're trying to punish me for not dropping everything the second you say you want me. Shit… what the *entire* fuck?"

Eventually, the door closed behind her with a soft click, but the silence it left behind was deafening.

I sat there for a while—wrapped in the blanket that still smelled like her skin—staring at nothing in particular. Just the stillness. Just the echo of what we used to be ringing in my ears. My body was still buzzing from her touch, but my heart... my heart was somewhere between heartbreak and survival mode. Again.

How did we end up back here?

She was always the storm and the calm that followed. Imani never walked into a room quietly—she entered like a question I never knew how to answer. And now here I am, asking myself all over again: What do I *want?* What do I *deserve?*

She said she wasn't counting us out. But she also wasn't choosing me.

Not now. Maybe not ever.

And the worst part? I *get* it. I really do. Life is messy. Timing is cruel. People don't always come back to pick up where you left off. Sometimes they just show up to remind you how much it hurt when they left.

I keep thinking about Kevin. Sweet, steady Kevin. He's the kind of man who brings peace instead of chaos. The kind who doesn't make me question my worth in the quiet moments. And yet... he's not the one I ache for in the dark. Is that fair to him? Is it fair to me?

I don't know.

All I know is... I'm tired. Tired of chasing moments that feel like home but never offer me a key. Tired of romanticizing pain and calling it passion. Tired of confusing history for destiny.

I want love that stays.

And maybe... just maybe, that starts with me staying with *myself.*

*****

It had been two days since Imani walked out of my apartment, and the energy she left behind still lingered like incense that refused to fade. In that short amount of time, every corner of my home felt like it had a memory with her stitched into it—her laughter in the kitchen, her scent on my pillow, the echo of her voice. She was everywhere and nowhere at the same time.

I hadn't called or texted. And to my surprise, she hadn't either. And now she was gone.

I wasn't angry anymore. Just… suspended. Hovering in that space between healing and holding on.

I took my journal from the nightstand and opened to a blank page. Kevin had texted me twice since that night, and I hadn't responded. Not because I didn't care. But because I didn't want to bleed old wounds onto something—someone—that hadn't even had the chance to bloom yet.

"Where do I go from here?" The first words landed on the page, but nothing followed them.

Maybe that was the real question. Not "who do I choose," or "what if Imani comes back." No. The question was about *me* and whether I was finally ready to choose myself—for once, without guilt, without the pull of old lovers and half-finished stories.

I closed my eyes and breathed deeply. I started to imagine a life where I wasn't waiting for someone to come back. A life where I didn't need to be someone's exception or unfinished business. A life that felt *whole*, even when it was quiet.

Maybe that meant having an honest conversation with Kevin. Maybe that meant learning how to be still with myself. Maybe that meant letting go of the idea that love has to come with a side of suffering.

I stood up, stretched, and walked to the window. The sunlight filtered in just the same as it had that morning with Imani. But this time, it felt like it belonged to *me*.

Maybe that was the beginning of something. Not with Imani. Not with Kevin. But with Serenity.

8

I decided to take the train back home to Baltimore, craving the slow rhythm of the rails to clear my thoughts. When I arrived, an Uber drove me through the familiar streets until we pulled up in front of a weathered brick bungalow on the South Side—a place that looked like it had witnessed both whispered confessions and quiet comfort, the kind of house that kept its stories tucked behind shuttered windows and ivy-covered walls. The lawn was manicured, a pair of wind chimes dancing lightly in the breeze. I stood there for a moment, heart thudding in my chest, wondering if this was even a good idea.

Amanda answered the door before I could knock — as if she'd been waiting for me all morning.

"Serenity," she said, softly. "You look so much like your mother."

I bit the inside of my cheek. "Thanks. She was beautiful."

"She really was."

We hugged. Amanda smelled like lavender and frankincense — a scent that hit a place in me I didn't know still had access to my childhood. We sat down in her kitchen, over tea and a plate of almond cookies she claimed she wasn't supposed to eat.

I didn't know how to begin, but I also didn't want to waste time.

"I've been thinking a lot about my mom lately," I said. "About her life. What she never told me. What she might've kept from all of us."

Amanda nodded slowly. "That's fair. Your mom… she kept a lot inside."

I glanced out the window, the words catching in my throat before I let them go. "I used to think she stayed with my dad because she was scared. But then she packed us up, left him, and even after he died… she still faded. Like something inside her had already gone quiet. I blamed him for so long. But lately, I've started to wonder—what if there were parts of her life I never really saw? Parts I never understood?"

Amanda sipped her tea and looked at me like she was measuring how much to say.

"There was a lot about your mom that most people didn't know. She loved you fiercely. That's the one thing that was never hidden."

There was a long pause.

"Can I ask you something personal?" I said, unsure of how to phrase what had been sitting in my chest for years. "Were you and my mom ever… together? Romantically?"

Amanda didn't flinch. She smiled — a tired, bittersweet smile.

"Your mom and I loved each other. Deeply. But it was complicated. She was terrified of what it would mean — for you, for her church, her family. For her own safety, frankly."

I nodded slowly. I had suspected for years, but hearing it said aloud made my throat tighten.

"Why didn't she ever tell me?" I whispered.

"Because she knew how much you already carried as a child. She didn't want to make your life heavier. And, if I'm being honest… she was afraid you'd stop loving her."

I shook my head, fighting tears. "That would've never happened."

Amanda reached across the table and took my hand. "I know. But trauma makes people believe the worst things about themselves."

Silence settled between us before Amanda finally spoke, her voice low and careful.

"There's something you should know," she said. "Your mom… she was planning to come be with me. She packed a bag once, even wrote me a letter.

I told her I'd help take care of her—and you, and your brothers. But she never went through with it."

Amanda looked away for a moment, as if searching the past.

"I was ready for more with her. But she couldn't bring herself to choose it. After that, our contact faded. Years passed. And still, I kept hoping—hoping one day she'd call and say she was on her way."

She paused, eyes wet.

"She never did. Instead, I got your call. You told me she'd died from a stroke."

I stared at her, stunned.

"You're saying… the day I called you—that was the first time you'd heard anything about Mama? Since she was planning to leave and come be with you?"

Amanda nodded.

"And she was going to come to you?"

"She was. We had made plans."

I felt like the wind had been knocked out of me. I stood up, pacing her kitchen floor.

"I've hated my father for so long. I've carried that blame like religion. And now you're telling me she was ready to start over? That maybe she actually wanted more for herself?"

"She did, Serenity," Amanda said softly. "She just… never could bring herself to put herself first."

I sat back down, this time feeling both hollow and full all at once.

"She would've loved Imani," I said, almost laughing through my tears.

Amanda smiled again. "From what I know about your mom, and from what I just saw in your eyes when you said that name… yeah. I think she would've."

*****

The train ride home felt like floating underwater. I couldn't remember when I started crying — it was somewhere between boarding and the memory of my mother folding laundry in silence. I wanted to scream, but my voice was buried under the weight of everything Amanda had just told me.

She was going to leave—really leave—and pack us all up to go live with Amanda.

She was finally choosing herself.

But she never did. Whatever hope she had slipped through the cracks of hesitation and time—and eventually, she died.

I walked into my apartment and stood in the doorway, unsure what to do with myself. The air felt stale, like it had been waiting for me to return with the truth.

I poured a glass of wine I didn't want and sat cross-legged on the floor in my living room, my phone resting silently next to me.

I wanted to call Imani.

I wanted to tell her everything — about my mother, about Amanda, about how my heart had been split open and stitched back together in the same hour. But I didn't. Because Imani wasn't my answer. Not now.

Instead, I pulled out one of the few photo albums I had of my mom. In one photo, she and Amanda were standing in front of the Washington Monument — laughing, sunglasses on, wind blowing through their hair like they were in a damn perfume commercial. There was so much joy in that image, it hurt.

They looked free.

I ran my fingers over the image and whispered, "You were going to choose yourself. I'm sorry you didn't get the chance."

The words tasted like forgiveness — not just for her, but for myself too.

I grabbed my journal and started writing, something I hadn't done in weeks:

> *Maybe loving someone isn't about getting the ending you want. Maybe it's about honoring what was real, even if it didn't last.*
>
> *Maybe I need to stop expecting people to come back to me whole.*
>
> *Maybe I have to be the one to choose me now.*
>
> *Maybe… it's time to live the life my mother didn't get to.*

The tears came again, but this time they weren't out of grief. They were release. They were a promise.

I looked around my apartment — at the canvases leaning against the wall, at the unopened piano keyboard still in its box, at the untouched fabric I kept saying I'd sew into something one day. I had been waiting to feel alive again. Waiting for Imani to show me how.

But maybe it was on me now.

I picked up my phone. I didn't call Imani.

I called a real estate agent.

"Hi… yes. I'm considering relocating. Possibly to Scottsdale."

Because maybe I didn't need to chase Imani.

Maybe I just needed to chase the version of myself I left behind there.

*****

It had been three days since I saw Amanda. I hadn't spoken to Imani. I didn't feel angry anymore — just… emptied. Like my heart had been cracked open, cleaned out, and now there was space. Real space.

For clarity.

For truth.

For something I could actually build on.

Kevin had called twice and texted me once — something simple like:

"Hope you're good. Thinking about you."

It was his way. Soft persistence. Not overbearing. Not chasing. Just present.

I sat in my kitchen, the same one where Imani and I had damn near turned the counter into a makeshift altar of lust and memory. But now, it was just a kitchen again.

I brewed coffee and thought about Kevin.

The way he brought me those calla lilies, how he listened when I talked about my mother, how he never flinched when I told him I wasn't ready to define anything yet.

And that ankh necklace. God, that necklace.

It wasn't just a gift — it was his way of saying, *I see you. And I want more of you.*

Maybe I had spent so long romanticizing unfinished business — with my mother, with Imani — that I had forgotten what it felt like to be met, right here, right now, in the present.

Kevin wasn't perfect. He was still trying to figure out what it meant to be a father—stumbling through it like many others. He had his own work to do, his own healing to face.

But he wasn't dragging me through his chaos. He was making room for me in it.

There was something beautiful about that.

I grabbed my phone and texted him:

"Hey… I've been doing a lot of thinking. Want to come by tonight? I'd like to talk."

He responded almost immediately:

"Of course. Whatever you need."

That was the thing about Kevin — he showed up. No drama. No riddles. Just a man who was emotionally available and emotionally mature. And yet, I had spent so much time chasing what felt urgent, magnetic, complicated…

But maybe love isn't always loud.

Maybe real love is patient and grown and willing to build, not just burn.

That evening, Kevin showed up with Ethiopian takeout and a bottle of red. He kissed my forehead before he said a word.

We sat on my couch, legs tangled like we had done before, only this time, I was fully here.

No ghosts in the room.

Just him.

Just me.

"I need to be honest with you," I said, my voice low but firm. "I've been carrying a lot. About my mom. About my past. And honestly… about Imani."

Kevin didn't flinch. He nodded, silently urging me to continue.

"We saw each other. It brought up a lot. And it helped me realize that I've been living in this loop — of unresolved stories and old fantasies. But that's not where I want to live anymore."

He looked me in the eyes. "So where do you want to live?"

I took a deep breath. "In the present. With someone who makes me feel safe. With someone who is actually *here*."

A beat passed. He reached for my hand.

"Okay. I'm here. Let's figure this out — together."

And in that moment, I knew:

I didn't have to chase magic.

I could *choose* stability.

And maybe, just maybe…

stability could be magic too.

We sat in a comfortable silence after dinner, the kind that wraps around you like a soft blanket. The wine was half gone, and the hum of the city filtered in through my window, distant and unbothered. Kevin leaned back, his arm draped along the back of the couch, his fingers lightly brushing my shoulder.

I took a breath.

"There's something I've been thinking about," I said carefully.

He glanced at me, attentive but relaxed. "Okay."

"I've been considering moving back to Scottsdale," I said, not making eye contact at first. "It's not a definite thing, but it's been on my mind. I've been craving something that feels more like me," I said quietly. "More space. More sun. And after talking with Amanda… I don't know. I just feel like being closer to the places that once gave me peace might help me figure out where I'm supposed to go next."

I finally looked at him. "I know your daughter is here, and that's huge. And I would never ask you to choose between her and me, but… I guess I'm wondering if that would be a deal breaker."

Kevin sat still for a moment, then shifted toward me. "Serenity, I love that you're thinking about your life like this — intentionally. That's part of why I'm so into you."

He reached for my hand.

"I'm just starting to get to know my daughter, yeah. And I'll keep building that relationship no matter where I live. But I'm also not going to put my life on hold to be geographically loyal to a situation that doesn't require that kind of rigidity."

I blinked, a little stunned.

"I'm not the kind of man who thinks being a father means becoming a martyr. It means being consistent. Showing up. Loving hard. And I can do that from anywhere, especially if it means creating something solid with *you*."

I searched his face, trying to make sure I wasn't hearing what I wanted to hear instead of what he was *actually* saying.

"You're saying you'd move? With me?"

He smiled. "I'm saying let's figure it out together. If Scottsdale feels like the next chapter for you, I'm open. I want us to *build* Serenity. Not just exist. And if that starts in the desert, I'm down to pack sunscreen and make it work."

My eyes welled unexpectedly.

Because for once, love wasn't asking me to choose.

It was offering to *go with me*.

Wherever I needed to go.

9

The sun was flirting with the Harlem skyline, dipping low and casting long golden beams across the redbrick buildings. Me and Cynthia strolled past the corner fruit stand on 125th, dodging a group of teenagers on scooters and the rhythmic beat of a conga player posted up outside a bodega.

"You really did it, huh?" Cynthia said, adjusting her sunglasses as she looked over at me. "You're actually moving back to Scottsdale. With *Kevin*."

I smiled, a little shyly, and nodded. "Yeah… it's official. We talked it through. He's coming with me."

Cynthia let out a long, dramatic sigh and threw her arm around my shoulder. "Damn, girl. I'm gonna miss your ass. But I can't lie—I'm happy as hell for you."

"I'm gonna miss you too. Like, *bad.*" I laughed, leaning into Cynthia's embrace. "You've been my sanity, my comedy, my late-night wine whisperer. Things won't feel the same without our post-work venting walks."

"Well, FaceTime better be on standby," Cynthia said, mock stern. "But for real though… I love that you chose him. And more importantly, that you chose *you*. 'Cause I see the shift in you, Poodah. You're glowing. For real."

I took a deep breath as we passed a small park, the scent of honeysuckle lingering in the air. "It's crazy. I was so torn, wondering if he'd even consider leaving. I didn't want to ask. Didn't want to *need* him to prove anything. But he brought it up before I could."

"He did?" Cynthia blinked.

"Yeah. He told me he's gonna keep showing up for his daughter, but he's not about to let the *possibility* of something real with me slip through his fingers either. He said he's been building his business for freedom—not just success. And now that he's got it, why not live fully?"

"Well, shit," Cynthia said with a satisfied grin. "A grown-ass man with vision and follow-through? That's sexy."

"I know, right?" I chuckled. "I've spent so much time trying to untangle the past. And now, it's like… I'm choosing peace. Space. Sunlight. I want to breathe again. And he wants to build something with me, not just around me."

We slowed at a crosswalk, watching as an older couple holding hands strolled ahead of us. Cynthia squeezed my hand gently.

"You deserve that kind of ease, babe. And I think your mom would be proud of the woman you've become."

I smiled but didn't speak. The warmth in my chest was enough for now.

As we crossed the street, I turned my face up to the fading light, heart steady, footsteps sure.

I was moving forward—and this time, it felt just right.

*****

That night, I walked alone through Fort Tryon Park, letting the hush of the trees and the distant hum of the city settle around me. The skyline sparkled just beyond the Hudson, and the breeze carried the faint scent of magnolia and damp earth.

I had come here countless times to think, cry, breathe. This was my place. A sacred pocket of the city where I could hear myself.

I slowed near the stone wall that overlooked the river, resting my hands on the cool surface. The lights from the George Washington Bridge twinkled in the distance like a promise.

My breath misted lightly in the evening air, even though fall was just around the corner.

I slipped my hand into my jacket pocket and drew out a small slip of paper—the note Amanda had left me after our last visit. On it, in Amanda's elegant handwriting, were the words my mother used to say when she needed courage: *"Trust what you know in your bones, even if your head hasn't caught up yet."*

I held it tightly, then closed my eyes and whispered softly, "Thank you, Mama."

No tears. Just stillness. A reverence.

The wind picked up slightly, brushing against my curls like a mother's hand. I smiled and turned, letting the moment imprint itself on me. One last inhale. One last look.

Then I walked toward the park exit, toward the subway, toward goodbye—but with no grief this time.

Just gratitude.

Because New York had held me when I needed holding.

But now it was time to let the sun do the same.